"What Are You Doing Here, Gideon?"

Lacey asked. "You're the last person in the world I expected to see."

"I spend my summers here. Always. I have, ever since we last met. Didn't you know? . . ."

She shook her head, truly surprised, her composure shaken. So *that* was why Aunt Edwina had discouraged her return! "No. No, I didn't . . ." Her voice trailed off as their eyes met and held. The unspoken memory of the past hung between them.

ABRA TAYLOR

was born in India, where her father, a doctor of tropical medicine, treated both maharajahs and British viceroys. Exposed to exotic places and unusual people from an early age, she developed an active imagination and soon turned to writing. The author of numerous romances, she is today a beloved storyteller, whose books are sought after by fans worldwide.

Dear Reader,

Thank you so much for the many letters I have received from you praising our Silhouette Special Edition series. Your comments and views have proved to be very informative and have been a great help to us in establishing Special Edition as a firm favourite amongst romance readers.

Special Editions have all the elements you enjoy in Silhouette Romances and more. These stories concentrate on romance in a longer, more realistic and sophisticated way, and they feature greater sensual detail.

I hope you enjoy this book and all the wonderful romances from Silhouette.

Please continue sending your suggestions and comments by writing to me at this address:

Jane Nicholls
Silhouette Books
PO Box 177
Dunton Green
Sevenoaks
Kent
TN13 2YE

ABRA TAYLOR

Forbidden Summer

Published by Silhouette Books

Copyright © 1984 by Abra Taylor

Map by Ray Lundgren

First printing 1984

British Library C.I.P.

Taylor, Abra
    Forbidden summer.—(Silhouette special edition)
    I. Title
    813'.54[F]   PS3570.A92/

    ISBN 0 340 36168 9

---

*The characters and situations in this book are
entirely imaginary and bear no relation to any real
person or actual happening*

Printed and bound in Great Britain for
Hodder and Stoughton Paperbacks, a
division of Hodder and Stoughton Ltd.,
Mill Road, Dunton Green, Sevenoaks,
Kent (Editorial Office: 47 Bedford
Square, London, WC1 3DP) by
Richard Clay (The Chaucer Press) Ltd.,
Bungay, Suffolk

Other Silhouette Books by Abra Taylor

Silhouette Special Edition
Season of Seduction
Wild Is the Heart
A Woman of Daring

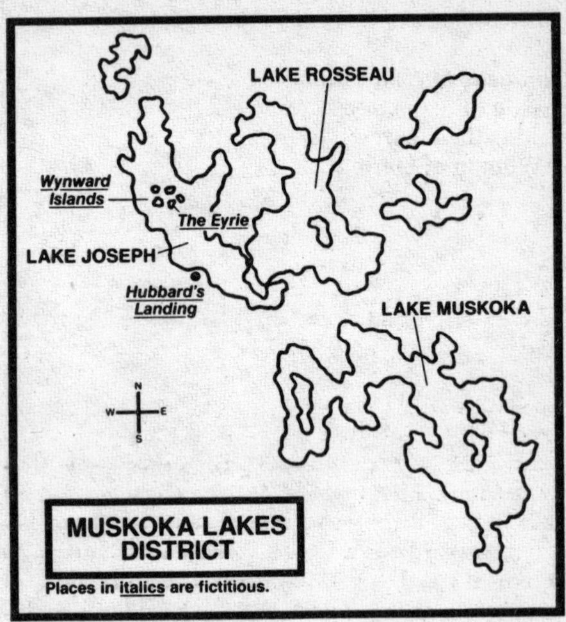

LAKE ROSSEAU
Wynward
Islands
The Eyrie
LAKE JOSEPH
Hubbard's
Landing
LAKE MUSKOKA
N
W E
S
MUSKOKA LAKES
DISTRICT
Places in italics are fictitious.

Chapter One

The Eyrie was just as Lacey remembered it from her seventeenth summer, a dark green mound rising out of the dark Muskoka waters. It was the largest of a group of smaller, similar islands the Wynward group, as it had come to be known back at the turn of the century, with a name honoring its earliest cottager, Lacey's great-great-grandfather.

As the marina's launch spanked over the ruffled waters, Lacey tried for detachment. July had made a good start with a brisk, sunny day, but the wind was very high. Pushing her whipping black hair from her eyes, she fought away the more disturbing memories of her last visit to Canada. She reminded herself that she was no longer a vulnerable teenager; that eight years had turned her into a full-grown woman with lots of defenses against the painful past. It had to be thrust from her mind. And it would be, she promised herself—as soon as this remote ten-acre island she owned ceased to be one of her headaches.

Almost all of the Eyrie was a tangle of thick vegetation and pine trees, the darkness of its aspect somewhat relieved by the sparkle of sun on restless lake water, a few stands of silver birch and sugar maple, and the occasional rough outcropping of rusty pink pre-Cambrian rock typical of this part of Ontario. A huge, aged, dark frame cottage dominated one of the island's protected inlets, with the boathouse and docks directly beneath it. The enormous, dilapidated structure was the only building in view on this approach to the island, and it stood as a sagging memory of palmier yesteryears in the Wynward family.

The marina owner, who had agreed to ferry Lacey to the Eyrie, was a crusty old-timer she remembered vaguely from her former stays in Muskoka. He hadn't seemed to remember her. He moved a wad of chewing tobacco from his wrinkled left cheek and spat sideways into the water, practiced enough not to choose the upwind side of the marina launch. Then his weatherbeaten eyes squinted at the cottage. "Could use a coupla hunnerd gallons o' paint on the trim!" he shouted above the engine, in a considerable understatement. "Turrible, way you Wynwards have let the old place go to wrack and ruin."

Hobie Hubbard was a straight speaker, as Lacey had already learned. "Blame thing is a disgrace to the lake, if truth be told," he had scolded only fifteen minutes earlier, when she had sought his help at the marina. "Fact is, I been itchin' to tell you some home truths for years. Ole Miz Wynward, she allus used to say, speak to the owner, an' that's the *young* Miz Wynward, my great-great-niece of the Pittsburgh Wynwards. *She's* the one got all the Wynward inheritance, now that her daddy's laid up with a stroke. *She's* the head of the Wynward family now. Well, now I got you here, young Miz Inheritance Wynward, I aim to speak my piece."

"Please call me Lacey," she had requested. "It's less confusing."

"Lacey?" He had ruminated for a moment. "Used to be some Laceys around these parts. You named after yer great-great-grandma?"

"Yes, Abigail Lacey, wife of the first Wynward. Aunt Edwina's mother."

"Aye. Well . . . should be ashamed o' yerself, young Miz Inheritance Lacey Wynward, living high on the hog off there in the Yew-nited States, while an ole lady like Miz Wynward ain't got two cents to rub together up here in Canada. A pensioner too. An' I ain't even tole you about that musty little room in the boardinghouse in town, where she lodges in wintertime. 'Spose you thought she could eat air, or did you jest ferget she lived up here in what I reckon you call the sticks? Imagine, the Eyrie rotting where she stands, with you sitting on that big pile o' cash your great-great-granddaddy made in coal. When your ole, ole auntie still summers in the place! There's more'n one person on this lake remembers how you Wynwards used to splash money around, like it was water. Hurt you, would it, to spend a few pennies on repairs fer your own flesh and blood?"

Lacey was accustomed to the misapprehension about the family wealth and would have corrected it if she had been anywhere except in Aunt Edwina's home territory. She kept her counsel, not feeling it was Hobie Hubbard's business to know that, under the terms of her grandfather's will through which she had inherited the cottage, repairs should have been Aunt Edwina's responsibility—not that Aunt Edwina could afford them now; she had long since gone through her patrimony. Nor could Lacey herself afford the necessary improvements, although she had been paying the huge mortgage and the hefty property taxes for years, along with the costs of a few absolutely essential repairs. A new septic system, at nearly ten thousand dollars, had been just one of these. The cottage had not only bled her dry, it had put her into debt.

As Hobie Hubbard slowed to come in for a landing, he squinted up at the tired timbers of the enormous wide-spreading structure that overhung the boathouse. Lacey was looking too. The projection of the casement window sagged badly; here and there the nonessential gingerbread decoration had broken away and had not been replaced; the white paint on the trim had peeled to the point of virtual nonexistence; and by the looks of it, the patched roof probably leaked even more badly than it had leaked eight years before.

The two boathouse doors were closed. Hobie steered in a great slow arc toward the strip of open dock that ran like a narrow boardwalk along one side of the structure, cutting his speed dramatically in order to allow the backwash to travel ahead of him.

He muttered some more dire utterances about the low state of affairs on the island. Lacey, too, was shocked to see the deterioration: unwashed windowpanes, dingy curtains, and a door swinging on a broken hinge suggested that things had come to a low pass indeed. Eight years before, the place had been seedy but clean—sparkling windows, freshly pressed flocked curtains, masses of petunias in the rock garden, and geraniums in the window boxes of the boathouse. Now these charms had vanished. But if Lacey's aunt was in truly reduced straits, she had certainly never mentioned it in her letters.

"Aunt Edwina always used to have summer help," Lacey said, worried. "Hasn't she had any recently?"

"Yup," Hobie Hubbard said. "Jest one nowadays, though. Reckon she couldn't afford all them armies o' college kids no more. Some years now, she ain't had no maids a-tall, jest one lone feller. Nice young feller too. What with them ole antique boats actin' up, an' with roof repairs an' dock work, she sure couldn't do without him. But he cain't do all of it, fer he ain't paid help, an' there's more'n enough fer one pair o' hands. Truth is, Miz Lacey, this ole place needs some locals on the job. Roofers. Painters. Plumbers. You aimin' to fix 'er up some, now that the ole lady's been took to hospital? Got me a brother-in-law down Bracebridge way. Odd jobs and such like. He kin give you a price."

"I won't be doing anything immediately," Lacey told him firmly. And when I do, she thought to herself, I won't be fixing it up. I'll be selling it. She would have done so years before, but her grandfather had left the Eyrie—his only bequest of value, as it turned out—to her with the proviso that the land be preserved if possible for his elderly aunt's use during her lifetime. By now Aunt Edwina had reached a very advanced age indeed. She was the firstborn and only remaining offspring of the five children produced by the first Wynward, Josiah Wynward, the coal baron who had married Abigail Lacey, bought the Eyrie, and founded the Wynward clan.

Lacey turned her eyes in the direction of the narrow strip of dock where they were now gliding almost within touching distance. To her surprise and relief, she saw that someone had replaced the treacherous, rotting, slime-covered planks on which she had broken her ankle at the age of seventeen. The job was passable if not perfect, but then university students weren't expected to have a degree in carpentry. In the old days Aunt Edwina had always managed to find masses of university students for summer help. The males had lived in the servants' bunkhouse on the high knoll at the far end of the island, while the females had stayed in some of the cottage's many bedrooms. Aunt Edwina, whose circumstances had been less straitened at the time, had paid the maids some kind of pittance, but the college boys had done the odd jobs around the Eyrie for nothing, because the arrangement gave them a free place to live while they ran a water-skiing school elsewhere on the lake. There had been seven or eight students during that last summer . . . but that was long in the past, and Lacey didn't want to think about it now. She tried to let the wind blow the memories from her mind.

Hobie Hubbard pulled in alongside the dock and cut the motor. Lacey jumped out, nimble and slender in her green linen slacks, while he thrust a couple of large suitcases onto the dock. "Truth is, Miz Lacey, you ain't goin' to be able to run them antique boats in the boathouse," he said. "Fer six, seven years I ain't bin too happy about touching the work on those things, except to put 'em up for the winter an' fill 'em up on credit. Your aunt, she ain't paid her bill fer going on ten years."

"Oh," Lacey said, her heart sinking. She didn't dare ask how much.

"I wouldn't of given her credit a-tall, if it wasn't a Wynward charge. Reckoned it'd all be settled someday." He paused and added idly, "You figgering to settle?"

"Er . . . of course."

He looked relieved, but fortunately didn't press for immediate payment. "Well then . . . when you git in trouble, Miz Lacey, jest call the marina. I kin sell you a real nice little inboard, something new an' easy to handle. Might even trade you even fer the Ditchburn, that big old mahogany wreck of a thing. Favor to old Miz Wynward."

"I think I can manage."

Old Hobie looked skeptical. "That Ditchburn, she's a caution to dock. An' the little Dippy—that's the dispro, the disappearing-propeller boat—she's a grand little boat, but right now she ain't running worth a hoot."

Lacey smiled. "I remember. I ran them both eight years ago. I loved them, especially the Dippy."

"Eight years?" Hobie snorted. "Well, you ain't seen 'em today. That Dippy, she's conked right out. An' the ole Ditchburn may have been a fine thirty foot of boat in her day, but she needs a new bottom. Dry rot in the timbers. Rusty bilge pump too. That young feller lives at the other end of the island, even *he* don't try foolin' with those old things too often nowadays. Runs his own boat. You'll see it in the boathouse, along of the others. So like I say, when you decide you need somethin' new, keep Hubbard's Happy Landing Marina in mind. Or if them ole boats won't start, jest phone fer a ride."

Lacey laughed. "I haven't forgotten how to canoe," she said.

"Ole canoe leaks, too, shouldn't wonder." Hobie took one last lugubrious look at the cottage and shook his head sadly. Then he reached for his ignition. "Give you a good price on a new bottom fer the Ditchburn," he said hopefully. "Fix up the engine. Build a new canopy. Refinish the top. She'll be like new."

"No, thank you," Lacey said politely but firmly. Eight years before, her aunt had been entertaining grandiose visions of having the long, stately old mahogany boat redone. The quote then had been ten thousand dollars for the bottom alone, and that didn't include mechanical work or the refinishing of the top. And after eight years of inflation, heaven alone knew what the quote would be. Lacey certainly didn't want to know.

"Well, best be off." Hobie managed one guarded yellow grin, his first of the day, before he took off.

When he had gone, Lacey picked up her suitcases and walked into the cottage, using the entrance through the boathouse. The two antique boats, one huge and one small, sat in the slips, their once-beautiful patina long since weathered away, the varnish blistered, the chromed metalwork pitted with age. A jaunty high-powered orange runabout, just the sort of thing a college student might want to race around in, shared the slip with the small disappearing-propeller boat, the Dippy as it was known locally, which was an antique oddity of the Muskoka lakes, with its single-cylinder engine situated smack in the middle. The two looked incongruous bobbing end to end in the waves that washed under the boathouse door, reminding Lacey of the time Gideon had rescued her. She quickly averted her eyes and hurried to the stairs that led up into the main area of the cottage.

She was glad to see that the old broken handrail had been replaced, and that one of the stair risers was new. Someone had been making the most essential repairs, eliminating the more obvious hazards, even though not much heed had been given to the cosmetic appearance of the cottage.

The living room, directly above the boathouse, showed distinct signs of decay. Old watermarks from the leaky roof stained the cream-colored walls. The chintz slipcovers Lacey herself had made eight years before, while partially immobilized by her broken ankle, looked as though they had not been washed since. She was also disturbed to see ruffles of dust visible beneath the rattan frames of the furniture, and the once-white curtains were long overdue for a wash. They hung limply, soiled and heavy with years of neglect. It distressed her also to realize that Hobie Hubbard, along with every one of the locals, considered her directly responsible for the deterioration of Aunt Edwina's living conditions.

It was because Aunt Edwina had been deliberately fostering the wrong impression, of course. Pride and preservation of appearances at all costs were Wynward faults—or strengths, depending on one's point of view. Aunt Edwina would never have dreamed of admitting that the family fortune no longer existed, and hadn't existed for years. The Pittsburgh Wynwards hadn't had *real* money, big money, since the "dirty thirties," when they had had to sell their coal holdings at a loss in order to cover various unwise speculations. And they had had even less since the 1960s, when a violent fluctuation of the stock market had wiped away the last remnants of the once-great fortune. The legend of wealth, however, was perpetuated by the existence of a few libraries, a museum, a private school, and a planetarium that bore the family's name, and even more importantly, by Aunt Edwina herself. As the family historian, now nearly ninety years of age, she had gone through a considerable fortune in her time. It was because of long-ago extravagances that she now spent her latter years in shabby gentility, keeping up a front and pining for the lost glories of her youth. She mightn't be able to hide her own financial condition except by burying herself in Canada, but her fierce pride wouldn't allow her to admit that the rest of the Wynward family, along with all of its collateral branches, was not swimming in lucre.

As owner of the island, which had been evaluated at half a million dollars—minus mortgages, of course—Lacey thought she was probably the richest of the clan, and yet for years it had been a struggle to pay the upkeep and the property taxes. She would have sold it long ago—even the will didn't bind her into a financial commitment she couldn't afford—but she had always been restrained by a sense of duty toward the elderly great-great-aunt who, with all her faults, had been kind enough to give Lacey a holiday home several times during her youth, the longest of these visits being that last, memorable seventeenth summer.

With a sigh, Lacey carried her suitcases to one of the ten bedrooms, the same one she had used years before. She wrinkled her nose at the dust motes that floated in the air. She was troubled that she hadn't come north to see Aunt Edwina until her aunt was, according to the doctors, practically on the brink of death. She was also perturbed by the evident deterioration of her aunt's financial state, which she hadn't suspected. There were reasons for Lacey's laxness, of course. Her last experience in Muskoka had been extremely painful, so she'd had strong personal reasons for not wanting to return. For another thing, Aunt Edwina had always been adamant in saying that Lacey should stay away.

"Think of the trouble you got into last summer," she had written years before in her spidery, elegant hand. Like many of her generation, she was a dedicated correspondent. "Don't you dare come and visit me, Lacey, because I don't want you upsetting me anymore. And I intend to be upset with you until you find some young man of good family and good fortune. One of the Mellons would do, or a Vanderbilt of the right branch, or a Rockefeller. *Then* you can come and visit. And please don't send any more letters asking about *that boy*, Lacey my dear. I have absolutely no idea where he is. Probably living in penury somewhere, and still trying to write the great novel of the century. Of course, his mother's summer place is gone now, but you never know, he might come back to visit Muskoka at any time—the old cottagers *do* have a way of returning. Canada is the only place the two of you are likely to connect. So under the circumstances, don't you think it's wise to stay away? After all, you know it would never do to get involved—better not to even see him when you can't possibly explain a thing—and we can't blacken the Wynward name, can we?" The paragraph had trailed off delicately at that point. "Please, darling," she had finished, "remember you promised not to mention this to your father. I wouldn't want Jacob to think I'd broken my promise to keep silence. And he would be devastated if I had to tell him why."

There were other reasons that Lacey had not returned to the cottage she owned. Her father's stroke of several years before had resulted in a semiparalysis that had chained her to Pittsburgh for nearly all of the intervening years. Only recently, since redirecting her career toward selling industrial real estate, had she been able to afford the full-time male nurse that Jacob Wynward needed.

She had done extremely well in real estate. At least one rival agent had been heard to say rather snidely that it was because of her looks and her old family connections, but Lacey knew it was mostly because of plain gritty hard slogging. She did her homework, boned up on her clients' problems, followed up on every small lead, knew all the zoning bylaws and the properties available, and often impressed hard-bitten businessmen with her grasp of their particular needs. True, her engaging smile and her good looks did occasionally draw in a client, although her youth and her femininity were more often a handicap than an asset. Always she had to fight to prove her efficiency, and sometimes she had to fight to protect herself. After suffering through a year of bruises in vulnerable places, she had learned to tactfully hand the potential bottom-pinchers over to one of the firm's older male agents, who had been particularly helpful in getting her started in the field.

Lacey turned her attention back to the cottage, touring from room to room, allowing only the professional part of her mind to surface. Out of nostalgia, she would have liked to save the old family cottage if at all possible, but she didn't for a moment think it was possible. Since taking the course in real estate, she could look at it with the eyes of a practical businesswoman, seeing its state of advanced decrepitude instead of the whimsical, outdated, tatterdemalion charm that had appealed to her in her teens. The whole spread—huge living room, huge dining room, ten bedrooms, kitchen, pantry, sunroom, storage rooms, games room, cedar closets—was a grand relic of once-moneyed days, but it had long since gone to seed. Just like the Wynward family itself, Lacey reflected.

At last, having done the grand tour and un-packed, she made herself a glass of lemonade from supplies found in the freezer of the old refrigerator. Aunt Edwina's heart attack had been only days ago, and the summer home was still well stocked with food. The milk didn't even smell sour.

Exhausted by the long day of driving, and by the emotional strain of visiting the hospital to see Aunt Edwina along the way, Lacey didn't feel she could yet face up to the cleaning spree that was so desperately needed. She carried her iced drink into the living room. "Tomorrow," she promised out loud, speaking ruefully to a moth-eaten framed moosehead over the doorway, which desperately needed a return trip to the taxidermist. Stuffing drooled from its mouth, and its dulled, dusty glass eyes looked back at her in mute appeal.

So did the eyes of the dingy Wynward portraits hanging over the mantel of the huge, chin-high stone fireplace. They were photographic portraits, a series of ovals all arranged in one big oaken frame, with the large central oval being, naturally, the portrait of the founding Wynward, Lacey's great-great-grandfather. The glass over the photographs was filthy. Lacey didn't want to look at this reminder of her heritage, so she turned her eyes toward the casement window and the lake—Lake Jo, as it was affectionately known.

Of the three major interconnecting Muskoka lakes, Lake Joseph was the least densely populated. Long stretches of shoreline remained untouched. However, during the approach by boat Lacey had noticed that some modern, expensive cottages had been built on several of the neighboring islands in the Wynward group, and at least one of them looked to be very grand indeed. The neighbors, fortunately, were not visible from this side of the Eyrie. She was glad she could see only the lake, a stretch of water uninterrupted for nearly a mile, and, if she moved right into the projecting casement, a fringe of the Eyrie's own curving shoreline.

The casement was in fact a bay window overhanging the boathouse, with glass on three sides and a built-in window seat. But the Wynwards had always called it the casement, and in her mind, Lacey did too. Needing to be alone with her thoughts, she took her drink and curled into the sunny nook, where she had liked to sit and dream in that seventeenth summer of her life.

The seventeenth summer . . .

It was the year she had inherited the cottage, the year of her grandfather's death, the year of her father's third or fourth business failure, the year of her mother's desertion, the year of her parents' divorce. It had also been the year when Lacey had been trembling on the brink of a womanhood she didn't quite understand, in part because there had been no boys at the strict school she had attended until that time. She had known all the down-to-basics facts about sex—girlish whispers and giggles had taken care of that—but her real experience had been limited to a few hastily snatched kisses and awkward, innocent, adolescent gropings, done mostly on dance floors or lighted front porches. Her father had been fairly strict with her—trying to steer her away from his own rakish behavior, Lacey imagined. That year she had badly missed her mother.

The year had been distressing for her in another way too. She had been attending the Wynward Private Seminary for Young Ladies on a Wynward bursary established half a century before, and somehow the secret had come out. There had also been a small item in the paper, something about her father's business incompetence and unpaid back taxes. It was bruited about that Lacey's mother had run off because she could no longer bear the critical state of the family finances. Everyone who was anyone in the exclusive boarding school soon knew that Lacey wouldn't have been there if her father had had to *pay*. She hated being patronized. And so it had been a year of confusion for Lacey, who for the first time had begun to understand that it didn't much matter what your social background was, when everyone knew you were really as poor as a churchmouse. Now, as an adult, she could admit her family's financial inadequacies, but in those days she hadn't felt able to. The Wynward mania for preserving appearances at all costs had left its mark. Yes, it had been a year of confusion.

But most of all it had been the year of first love. The year of sweet awakenings and dashed dreams. The year of trembling adolescent yearnings and hopeless hopes. The year of pain . . . the year of Gideon.

Drifting, daydreaming with arms linked around her knees as she sat in the window seat, she could almost see him through half-closed eyes. It was through this very window that she had first sighted him. With heavy lashes veiling her vision to leave only shifting shapes of wind-stirred birches through the heavily smudged window, she could almost imagine him as she had first seen him then— pushing his way through the overgrown path from the other end of the island, shade dappling that lick of unruly hair that curved over his forehead, where sun had streaked the mid-brown almost to blond. He had been dressed in jeans and a loose white T-shirt—his long lithe body a little too skinny on first appearance, although she had later discovered there was a surprising muscularity to his lean young frame when she saw him stripped to a bathing suit.

She remembered his skin, warm and hard and firm, tanned to mahogany because of his summer occupation. She remembered the little sunburst of lines at the corners of his eyes. To Lacey's yearning heart so many years before, those little smile indentations had made him seem far more mature and experienced than his twenty-two years, and they had also had the effect of turning her seventeen-year-old knees weak with longing. So had his grin. It had been a lazy, mocking, teasing white grin that made her insides feel like mulled wine whenever he chose to confer it—which had been mostly on the other college students, some of them the female ones who served as summer maids to Aunt Edwina.

Gideon Jerrold had been the only American among the students running the ski school, and also the only nonstudent. His presence was explained because his mother's Philadelphia forebears, the Llewelyns, had been Muskoka cottagers since before the turn of the century. They had bought land about the same time as the Wynwards. Lacey remembered seeing the Llewelyn place in her early youth: it had been a spread typical of old Muskoka cottages, not dissimilar to the Eyrie, although in considerably better condition. Because Gideon's mother was widowed and a working woman, Gideon had summered there in boyhood, with his grandparents. Then the place had burned down. With no family cottage to stay in, Gideon had taken to staying with Lacey's Aunt Edwina during the summers while he was in college. On the year in Lacey's memory, he had already gained his degree in history, but with no steady job, he had returned to summer at the Eyrie. He had been trying his hand at writing, because he didn't want a career as a professor. "I'm not ready to settle down and make a living the hard way," he had said at one point.

That seventeenth summer was the first year Gideon and Lacey had actually met, although the families had known each other for many, many years. He had paid Lacey only the most casual of attentions, offhanded politenesses really, until the end of the season.

A case of chicken pox—a great embarrassment to a seventeen-year-old—had kept Lacey in Muskoka into the month of September. Gideon, alone of all those who had summered in the bunkhouse, was also still on the island. Aunt Edwina had kept him on because she liked to spend her autumns at the Eyrie and couldn't do so alone. Then, on what was to have been Lacey's last day in the northland, she had gone for a final spin in the unpredictable Dippy. It had been a few days after Labor Day, the lake virtually emptied of summer visitors, the boat traffic spookily nonexistent in the deserted back bay where the Dippy's antique motor had sputtered into silence.

Lacey had been stranded for hours, first while she tried to get the cranky old motor going, then while she attempted in vain to rouse an answer from the several locked-up cottages in sight. Each of them had been eerily empty. Finally, with no other boats in sight, she had started to paddle. It had turned cold and she had been shivering, with only a thin T-shirt and shorts to protect her. And when the silvery little tin boat, Gideon's own, had come out of a sunset horizon, he had seemed like a knight riding in a sheath of shining armor.

For a moment she had been tongue-tied. Then, wanting to seem casual, she had raised a hitchhiker's thumb. "Hi," she had said. "Going my way?"

"If you're going mine," he had said, with a smile that turned her heart inside out.

It had been a slow trip back, towing the skittish but irreplaceable antique Dippy with only a low-horsepower motor on a boat that was even smaller. They had talked, laughed, shivered, and learned a lot about each other. Gideon had been looking for Lacey for hours. He had had nothing to warm her but his own T-shirt, and when that hadn't worked, he had offered his body heat. He had suggested it with a light grin, but the lightness had soon vanished as they crouched together in the bottom of the cold tin boat. Lacey, whose adolescent heart had already done a considerable amount of pining over the course of the summer, had reached out hesitantly to touch his arm at one point, and the tentative, shy, unthinking gesture had changed the mood irrevocably.

And then . . . she could remember the way his brown eyes had darkened even before night fell, remembered the exact words he had muttered as he pulled into the boathouse, remembered the wild flutter of her heart and the heavy pulse of his, remembered the feel of his fingers winding in her hair and his lips moving so very, very gently over hers, touching and lifting as lightly as shadows shaking on a path. . . .

With a sudden start, she sat bolt upright in the window seat. Her eyes flew wide. That wasn't imagination out there, moving along the dappled path. That was a man. His progress behind the treed screen of the shoreline hadn't attracted her attention, for it had seemed but a figment of her own slow daydream. His sudden stillness, however, as he emerged from the trees had caught her eye. It had seemed to turn him solid. He had stopped to stamp out a cigarette on a rock before vanishing into the boathouse. His back was half turned and his head was bent, leaving his facial features unseen and heightening the impression of broad shoulders and long, rangy legs. And then he had swerved quickly and gone through the boathouse door, identity still concealed.

She had the crazy impression that it might have been Gideon, just from the controlled flow of those limbs. But of course that couldn't possibly be. This man had been far broader in the shoulder, more compact in the powerful line of the hip, and there had been no streaked blond in the bent brown head. Besides, Gideon didn't smoke—or he hadn't, back in those days. And after what had happened eight years before, Aunt Edwina wasn't likely to welcome him to the island. And yet, there was still that haunting feeling. . . .

It must have been this year's young college helper, the one old Hobie Hubbard had mentioned. The youth had the trim, tall, muscular build of a quarterback, which Lacey supposed accounted for the fact that some of the manual labor had been well done, even if the cosmetics of the cottage had been ignored, and even if the interior suffered from poor housekeeping. Scolding herself for an overactive imagination, Lacey turned her eyes out toward the water, thinking she would soon see the jaunty orange runabout backing out of the slip.

And yet, when she heard the footsteps coming with such assurance up the stairs, she knew it had to be Gideon. They were a man's footsteps, not a boy's. And they were Gideon's. No one else would walk right into the cottage as if he belonged. Odd how she remembered his measured pace after all these years. She didn't turn her head when he appeared in the doorway, because she wanted a moment or two to school her expression. His physical presence reached across the room, creating an electricity that sent strong charges of silent static through the air. Gideon, she thought to herself, Gideon, Gideon, Gideon . . . and the refrain was a wild, hurting hammering in her head and in her heart.

Gideon was more prepared for the moment than Lacey. Since the day of her aunt's coronary, he had half expected her. The island, after all, was hers; and other than her debilitated father, she was old Miss Wynward's closest relative. He had sighted the marina launch, seen the slim figure with the windblown black hair, heard the raised voices which often traveled to shore more loudly than the motor's roar, taken time to compose himself before coming to the main cottage. It hadn't been hard because he was sure he was completely over her. There had been other women in the intervening years, one or two he had even fancied himself in love with for a time. He thought himself totally hardened to Lacey Wynward, inured to all emotions except a cold sense of resentment that with a background of such family wealth she would have so little consideration for an elderly maiden aunt in such dire straits.

But now, with a sudden, surprising race of anger, he was thinking: how can she sit there with such nonchalance, such indifference? She must know it's me, or she would have turned her head to the door.

She must have seen me in the approach, for she's been staring out that casement window, curled into it as she had been fond of curling so many years ago.

At last she turned to face him and her small, cool smile angered him also. Could those be the same lips that had once trembled sensuously, swollen with his ardent kisses? "Hello, Gideon," she said, so calmly that he knew his arrival had been no surprise.

"You shouldn't be sitting in the window seat," he rasped, with a harsh depth to his voice that hadn't been there eight years before. "It's not safe. That whole overhang badly needs shoring up with new timbers."

She laughed, a husky, warm sound with just the tiniest edge of bleakness to it. It reminded him of banked log fires on a wintry night. "Gideon to the rescue again," she said lightly. "If the cottage can survive that high wind, I'm sure an extra hundred and fifteen pounds won't bring on a catastrophe." But she rose to her feet and started to move slowly into the main area of the living room.

He watched with hooded eyes, nothing in his grim expression betraying that she reached him in any way. And yet, despite the hardness in his heart, he felt the old tug of sexual attraction. He reminded himself that it was only the stirring of glands and hormones. It had nothing to do with love, which had died years before. It was the way she moved, of course: that graceful, flowing, self-assured way that came from innate good posture and a good—no, beautiful—figure. In eight years her body had ripened, become even lovelier with full maturity, although her waist and her legs were as slim as ever. There was breeding in every bone, every fluid movement, every graceful mannerism. Time had given a finer definition to the high cheekbones and the little hollows beneath them, and there was a stronger character written in the proud, delicate curve of her nostrils and jaw. He wondered how many men had kissed that jaw, and then realized, with a sharp sense of surprise, that despite her added veneer of composure, there was still an untouched look about her, as if she held something in reserve. An illusion, of course.

Was she still waiting for the right match? he wondered. Her aunt had said something about an engagement two or three years ago, and Gideon's pride had never allowed him to inquire whether it had resulted in marriage. He had told himself he didn't give a damn. Now he was curious. He could see no ring on Lacey's finger.

She was circling the room in silence, as if trying to decide which of the dilapidated pieces of furniture to sit down on. He watched in equal silence, not particularly caring if his lack of easy conversation disturbed her. How beautiful she was . . . and yet, when all was said and done, how shallow was the person beneath that beauty. She had the fine Wynward looks, but she also had all the Wynward flaws and faults and failings.

Her dark fringe of lashes veiled the large, translucent eyes that had once caused his breath to catch in his throat. Years ago, that day in the boat, she had remarked on the similarity of their eye color, and Gideon remembered laughing. "Mine are plain brown," he had said, "but yours . . . yours are like molten gold. No, I take that back. They're not so unsubtle. They're like polished brown mica, with a golden light shining through."

"Yours have golden flecks too," she had pointed out a little shyly, because they had only started to discover each other at the time.

The true discoveries had come over the course of the next few weeks. On returning to the Eyrie, she had caught her foot in a rotten timber on the old dock and had broken her ankle. The break had changed her plans for the autumn—which, as far as Gideon knew, included only a life of indolent ease, a debutante existence in the Pittsburgh social whirl. She hadn't been planning to finish her last year of high school or attend university, or so she had told him while he had been taking her to Bracebridge to get her leg x-rayed. "Wouldn't you know! Now that I've broken this darn thing, I doubt if I'll be able to get a job right away," she had said with a wince when he lifted her back into the car for the return trip to the island.

"Then relax and enjoy being an invalid," he had answered with a laugh. "I can't imagine your aunt Edwina approving of your working, anyway. *She* never did! I doubt your father would let you take a job, either."

"How on earth would you know? You don't know my father."

"Ah, but my mother's family did—the Llewelyns. In fact, they used to know him quite well when he was younger, back when he spent his summers up here. Tall, distinguished, and wonderfully handsome, my grandparents said, just like all the Wynwards. From what your aunt Edwina tells me, I have impressions of a rich, idle, charming gentleman of great breeding, who occasionally amuses himself by sitting at the head of a long board table, writing a check for charity, or clipping his unclipped coupons. I can't imagine *his* daughter working. And if you don't need to work, why work? I wish I'd been born to a life of indolence myself."

He still remembered the peculiar glance Lacey had shot him, but she hadn't mentioned career plans again.

The ankle cast had remained in place for several weeks. And so she had remained in Muskoka until autumn turned the shorelines to a blaze of crimson and orange and gold, a brilliant palette stained with the dark, changeless black-green of pines and firs and cedars.

And of course, he had had the ill chance to fall in love. It was only because they had been thrust together, he had told himself a thousand times since. He had fought the attraction at first. She was too young for him, and he was too young for marriage. He desired an affair, but avoided trying for one, partly because of that puppy-love look in her eyes. It had been there all summer long, giving her a vulnerability he could have taken advantage of, but didn't wish to. At twenty-two, he had been already confident and experienced in matters of sex—too confident and too experienced to be tampering with a vulnerable virgin who didn't even know much about kissing. He had learned that with just one kiss—a brief, testing caress in the boat on the day he'd gone looking for the Dippy. After discovering her ignorance, he had sworn to himself that he wouldn't take advantage.

And yet, during that autumn, there had been too

many occasions when he had had to catch her, when she stumbled on rocky ground in her ankle cast. Too many days when he had had to lift her into a boat, when her young, trembling body had clung helplessly against his. Too many nights when they were virtually alone on the island, their only chaperone a very elderly lady who had a habit of retiring when the first stars poked through the black velvet sky. There had been too many times when he had brushed Lacey's hand, locked his eyes with hers, lowered his face impulsively to drink in the fragrance of her hair and feel its gentle tickle against his nose. Often, it had been pine-scented from lying on a soft forest floor of old, fallen needles. Lacey had liked to lie back and look up through the trees. He remembered the way her young half-ripe breasts had pushed against her thin T-shirt, and how difficult it had been to keep his hands to himself.

He wrenched his mind back to the present and realized his eyes were on her hair. It was simply cut, still in a long swing that spilled over her shoulders, and wore a soft sheen of cleanliness. He used to think it looked like moonlight licking over the dark lake at midnight, when slow waves lapped the surface of the water. Once, Gideon hadn't been able to pull his eyes away, but now he could. He was more mature, immunized by time.

After circling restlessly for a few moments, Lacey came to a standstill quite near him and pushed the hair back behind one ear, a graceful mannerism he remembered from years ago. At the time he had thought it denoted unsureness. Now it seemed a sophisticated gesture and irritated him.

"What are you doing here, Gideon? You're the last person in the world I expected to see."

"I spend my summers here. Always. I have, ever since we last met. Didn't you know?"

She shook her head, truly surprised, her composure shaken. So that was why Aunt Edwina had discouraged her return! "No. No, I didn't. I would have thought . . ."

Her voice trailed off as their eyes met and held. The unspoken memory of the past hung in the air between them. "You mean on this island? My island?" she asked at last, and he could hear the difficulty in her uneven breathing. Was she remembering the past, then, just as he was?

"Yes, on your island." His voice became bitingly cynical, a defense against old hurts and old attractions. "I'm surprised your aunt has never mentioned it to you. Free lodging in exchange for a few odd jobs . . . yes, Lacey, I'm still the same ne'er-do-well I was then, a few years older but not much wiser. Still refusing to take a regular job. Still refusing to use my degree in history. Still writing. Your aunt gives me regular lectures on what a failure I am."

"Are you?" asked Lacey quietly, her eyes troubled.

"Critically, no. Financially . . . that's really none of your damn business, is it? I manage to survive well enough by my standards—but not, I suppose, by yours. But then, I don't set my sights quite so high as you do."

"You used to," she returned, remembering the times he had shared his hopes for the future.

"Then obviously," he bit back, "I've lowered them. I'm happy with a hand-to-mouth existence.

Can you think of any other reason I'd be hanging around here every summer, doing your aunt Edwina's odd jobs in exchange for free lodging? It's a damn good thing for your aunt that I do. Recently, with inflation and lack of family support, she hasn't even been able to afford university students. Me she can get for nothing, simply because I happen to like spending my long, lazy summers up in this neck of the woods. But then, you know all about that, don't you? Once a wastrel, always a wastrel. Those weren't your exact words, I know, but that's the general impression I got from your farewell note."

She ignored the sarcasm. "Then your fortunes haven't improved," she said simply, looking genuinely regretful for a moment. "I'm sorry to hear it."

He shot a scornful glance at her ring finger. "I see yours haven't, either. Still looking for a socially acceptable husband?"

"That's a low dig, Gideon," she said levelly.

"Someone who could support you in the style to which you had always been accustomed." He was mimicking Aunt Edwina's aristocratic accent. "I believe that's how your aunt put it at the time, just to fortify the things you implied in that stilted little letter to me. Would it have been so very hard to say good-bye to me in person?"

Her eyes darted away, and she licked her lips before answering. "Yes, it would, at the time. I had a silly teenage infatuation for you, Gideon." Her gaze moved back to meet his, very cool and guarded again. "I hadn't realized where it was leading until Aunt Edwina woke me up to my responsibilities. I realized I had to get away from you as fast as possible. It wasn't a suitable liaison."

"Liaison? I believe I offered marriage."

She answered very carefully. "Yes, I remember. You proposed when Aunt Edwina appeared to interrupt. To save my honor, wasn't it? That was very gentlemanly of you, Gideon. In any case, I thought it better to refuse. I owed it to the family to make a decent match."

"You really are a true Wynward, aren't you?"

"Yes," she said. Her shoulders looked a little too stiff, and perversely it pleased Gideon to realize she wasn't enjoying this encounter. He wasn't enjoying it either.

"In your aunt, that Wynward social nonsense is amusing. But in you—" He broke off abruptly, remembering that it would be better to keep his tone detached, if possible. "I take it you must be divorced?"

"No. I never married." She hesitated. "You?"

"I've never felt the need of a wife," he said casually, but with some deliberate cruelty. "I can get what I want without. Why take on the responsibility of marriage? If kids came along, I might actually have to work for a living. For years, Lacey," he added dryly, "I've been grateful to you for saving me from that particular fate."

"Gideon . . ." she started, but then bit her lip and fell into silence.

"My state of unmarital blessedness is natural," he continued indifferently, "but I'm not so sure about yours. Frankly, Lacey Wynward, you surprise me. In eight years you haven't managed to find a suitable candidate? One with all the right qualifications? As I can't imagine a lack of suitors, I have to imagine a lack of willingness on your part." His eyes glittered with faint scorn. "I heard you were engaged once; that's why I asked about divorce. Did you break it?"

She paused again before she said, "Actually, I've been engaged twice."

His brows lifted; that really did surprise him. "What happened?" he asked. "Fortunes not big enough? Blood not blue enough? Names not on the social register? Or did Daddy threaten to disinherit?"

Her lips compressed a little, and he thought he saw a wince of pain pass over her smooth brow. But her voice was well controlled when she spoke. "Why must you be so hurtful, Gideon? I've never wished you anything but well."

He uttered a short, harsh, humorless laugh, and the little golden flecks in his eyes blazed with sudden, angry, unconcealed contempt. "All the success in the world—yes, I believe that's what you did wish me in your note. And I suppose if I'd had it, you might have considered marrying me after all? I do have a few drams of socially acceptable blood in me, so I have to assume that my major lack was money. I used to wonder whether you'd come back if my name hit the best-seller list. Would a successful author have filled your qualifications for a husband? Don't bother answering that, for I'm no longer interested in knowing."

His answer was bitter, and the depth of the embitterment surprised even Gideon. It made him realize that, beneath the scar tissue, some of those old wounds were still painful.

Lacey made it clear that she didn't care to pursue

the question of the past. "I'll get you a lemonade," she said suddenly and stiffly, not making a question of it. Before he could refuse she had slipped quickly past him and vanished from the room. He didn't call her back because he needed a moment alone, to put reins on his unruly emotions. Why had he permitted his mask of indifference to crack like that?

He hated the fact that she could still affect him so. He supposed it was because the ending of their autumn romance had been so swift, so wrenching. At the time it had seemed as though a vital part of him had been rooted out without anesthetic.

In retrospect, he had realized that Lacey's ancient aunt must have been keeping a weather eye on the progress of the relationship. When hand-holding and hidden glances became obvious, she had become alarmed enough to change her sleeping routines. With the cast at last taken off, Lacey had become more mobile. And, driven by weeks of wanting and tentative touches, many of them initiated by Lacey herself, Gideon had become less able to control his passions. It was inevitable that sooner or later they would find their way to the bunkhouse after dark. The night they did, old Miss Wynward must have been keeping a close check on their movements. By flashlight she had picked her way up to the bunkhouse, where he and Lacey had slipped by starlight, and surprised them naked and twined together with desperate urgency in the dark. He had assured old Miss Wynward that his intentions were honorable; that he intended to offer marriage. That, of course, hadn't prevented Lacey from dressing in quick mortification and returning with her aunt to the main cottage.

And the next morning Lacey had been gone. She had taken the Dippy into town and caught the first bus out, leaving only that stiff, uncommunicative little note, and old Miss Wynward to tell him he would have to make his fortune first if he truly wanted to marry into the Wynward family.

"You don't have enough money for Lacey," she had said in her quavery old voice. "You know I'm very fond of you, Gideon. Why, I've known your family forever. But it would never, never do. Lacey now realizes that too. I reminded her that her father would disinherit her if she made such a terribly unsuitable match. If she were to marry you, she'd never own a thing but this island . . . you *do* understand, don't you? You're young, Gideon, you'll get over it, just as you got over that pretty college student you were embroiled with earlier this summer. And the other pretty one *last* summer. Oh, yes, I know about those things! I may be an old, old lady, but I still have two sharp eyes in my head. I can guess what goes on in that bunkhouse every year, now that I can't afford to hire a chaperone for the lot of you. If I didn't need the help so desperately I would never, never let you boys stay over there alone. You're not ready to settle down yet, young man, and you won't be ready until you get a decent job and a decent income and a decent *position* in the community. Lacey wants those things too. She simply lost her head for a little time—you know how impulsive young girls can be when they have these passing teenage crushes. And don't for a moment imagine that she's run away because of those other romances of yours. She doesn't know about them. She's gone simply because she came to her senses and realized she can't possibly get involved with an irresponsible wastrel who has no job plans, no future, and not even two pennies to jingle in his pocket. Oh, by the way, Gideon, when you go into town to tow the Dippy back, buy me a paper, will you? And one lamb chop. If that butcher gives you any nonsense about paying off the Wynward charge, don't put up with it. Tell him if he sends any more nasty letters I shall have to take my custom elsewhere."

He knew he would have to pay for the paper himself, and probably for the lamb chop as well. And she dared to talk to him about financial irresponsibility? If she hadn't been old, frail, and female, he thought he would have smashed his fist into her face. But in time he had cooled, because he was curiously fond of the pretentious old lady with her tattered dreams, and because her words only confirmed what Lacey had written in her letter.

Gideon's mind returned sharply to the present when Lacey returned with two fresh lemonades. She handed one to him, and he could sense her sudden tensing when their fingers touched briefly. The fleeting connection of their eyes seemed difficult for her too. She looked away quickly, and he wondered if there was a slight stain of embarrassment in the smooth golden skin over her high, elegant cheekbones. If so, he was glad to see it.

She went at once to perch on the arm of an overstuffed chair. "How's your mother?" she asked.

"Dead," he said curtly. "She died last year."

"I'm sorry."

That put a short brake on conversation, but eventually Lacey spoke again. "Your hair has darkened," she said in a distant voice, seeking an innocuous topic.

Gideon didn't want to prolong the encounter. He remained on his feet. "Age," he returned with a shrug. "And a different summer occupation. I'm not in the sun as much."

"You've broadened too."

"I'm no longer a boy."

"I saw that you fixed the dock, and I think you also did some work on the roof." She added with apparent sincerity, "Thank you. Those are big jobs, above and beyond the call of duty when you're not being paid."

"I only repaired the essentials." He scowled and took a deep draught of the lemonade, impatient to be gone as soon as possible. "As the island doesn't belong to me, I've had a limited interest in fixing it up."

"And you took Aunt Edwina to the hospital. Thank you for that too."

He glanced up, eyes narrowed. "You saw her?"

"Yes, I stopped off before coming here. One of the nurses told me you'd brought her in."

"How is she?"

"Comatose, under heavy sedation. Her condition is still critical, although it's stabilized somewhat."

By telephone, Gideon had already received the latest reports from the hospital, but that wasn't why he was asking. He forced himself to relax. "You weren't talking to her then?" he asked.

"Not really. She did wake for a moment, but she's not up to conversation. A few meaningless mutters, that's all. The nurse said to come back tomorrow."

"I might go with you." He placed the half-finished glass on a wicker table and wiped his mouth on the back of his hand, as if to remove the bad taste the whole encounter had left. "I must go. Will you excuse me?"

He strolled to the door and then he was gone. Lacey remained on her feet. Her fingers around the iced lemonade glass had turned numb from intense pressure on the hard, chilly surface. She heard his footsteps fade, heard the bang of a door down in the lower level of the cottage, heard the muffled sound of footsteps on rock. And then, almost without knowing she had moved, she found herself in the casement window, watching the Eyrie's path, with the trembling fingers of one hand pressed against a dirty pane.

She saw his slow tread and the tension in his shoulders. In moments he had passed the clearing and was half hidden behind a screen of birch and straggling cedar, glimpsed only intermittently, then growing small with distance as he wended his way toward the bunkhouse. Her eyes followed the dwindling shape until the only movements to be seen were the restless toss of branches in the wind and the stirring of their shadows on the path.

When even imagination could not produce the image of his vanishing form, she released the fierce clench of her teeth and uttered one strangled, almost inhuman cry. It released none of her emotions.

And so, with uncharacteristic desperation, she hurled her emptied lemonade glass at the great stone fireplace where the family portraits hung. "Damn you! Damn you! Damn you!" she cried, in an agony that encompassed all the Wynwards at large.

Chapter Two

With a fury almost equal to that with which she had hurled the glass, Lacey changed into old clothes and threw herself at some of the tasks she had intended to leave until the morrow, starting with the cleaning up of the shattered glass itself. It was a desperate effort to quell her thought processes. In physical exhaustion, she might find release from the old longings that oozed through her, like a new source of water trickling through the porous rock of a long-untapped underground spring. She should never have allowed herself that spell of wayward daydreaming in the window—it had made her too vulnerable in the unexpected moment when Gideon appeared.

Was that why she had felt the instant physical pull? The magnetic attraction? Gideon had changed enough that she felt she should have been able to think of him as a different person. The boy had gone, and she wasn't sure she liked the man who had taken his place. The boy Gideon had been careful, considerate, respectful, and always tender in the way he had handled her. The man Gideon had a streak of cynicism, a biting sarcasm, almost an emotional cruelty in his manner. Although she could understand some of the reasons for his resentment of her, she couldn't understand its depth. She felt that in eight years he should have come to terms with her departure. Especially since, as Aunt Edwina had pointed out at the time, there had been other females in his life. Among other things, Lacey's aunt had hinted at his various amorous exploits over the course of a few summers. At the time Lacey had wondered how she could ever have been so naive as to think she might have been a first love for him too. It had hurt, but it had been only the beginning of Aunt Edwina's dissuasions.

Lacey supposed Gideon hadn't changed much in respect to his appeal for women. Something he'd said today had implied that he didn't lack for female companionship. She wouldn't have expected him to; there was a physical dynamism about him. His frame was as lithe but far more powerful than it had been, and his face had filled out, too, giving him a mature attractiveness that had been only promised in the young, thin Gideon. His features had become more definite, his jaw harder and more squarely set. To counterbalance these positive assets, his expression was forbidding, his mouth more cynical. The little smile lines still fanned out from the corners of his eyes, but that was the only sign that he retained the sense of humor and enjoyment of living that had once caused her bones to liquefy. The wonderful lazy grin, if it still existed, had not once been seen during their encounter.

Well, if he saved it only for other women, that was all for the best. The last thing she wanted was a resumption of their old relationship. So why set him straight about some of the things for which he seemed to hold her in contempt? Let him keep his distance and she would keep hers, and no trouble would develop between them.

For nearly eight years Lacey had been trying to tell herself that the old attraction had been merely the result of youth, inexperience, and propinquity. Forever after that first brush with carnal knowledge, she had been doubly on guard with other men. Perhaps it was true that the two brief and inconclusive engagements had been attempts to marry according to her family's wishes, but even more they had been attempts to live a normal existence—to forget Gideon. Contrary to his cynical comment, the suitors would have been acceptable enough even by Aunt Edwina's impossible standards. Both were members of old Pittsburgh families. Lacey would never have broken the engagements, except, except . . .

She wasn't sure why she had broken them. The memory of Gideon? The tiny threads of doubt, encouraged by the shattering revelations of her seventeenth summer? The gleam of faint disapproval she thought she detected in her father's eye? By the age of twenty-three, at the time of her second engagement, Lacey would have put some direct questions to him, asked him if she had his approval for the marriage, if he had been able to answer. But he couldn't. His stroke had left most of his facial muscles paralyzed, left his vocal cords barely capable of speech. It had also affected his brain, leaving him confused, so that sometimes when he said yes, he meant no. Even if he had answered, he might have articulated wrongly.

Oh, God, how *could* she still be physically attracted to Gideon? Must feelings always be so ungovernable? Did logic exercise no control? A rage of physical activity was her only answer to the ferment of uncertainty that boiled and bubbled inside her.

By three o'clock in the morning she had cleaned out the living room, including the hazardous casement window, which she had walked right into and polished ferociously despite Gideon's warnings. She had laid out numerous baited traps in virtually every room of the house after seeing multiple mouse droppings here and there. She had made great piles of dirty curtains and dirty slipcovers to take to the laundromat in town. She had swept the living room floor and washed it, wiped the wicker furniture, and tried without success to scrub away the water stains on the wall. She had dusted the moosehead and shined its accusing eyes. She had even overcome her distaste for all things Wynward enough to give the portrait over the mantel a vigorous, thorough cleaning. She had struggled the big rag rugs out the door to the railing over the canoe slip, and beaten them in the dark with a paddle as if that could relieve her intense anger at fate. When she was finished, she didn't even have strength to carry the rugs back inside.

And that was only one room.

She fell onto a bed in her underclothes. She had removed her now-filthy jeans and shirt but couldn't bother to look for a nightie. Who needs a nightie anyway, was her last thought as she slipped into exhausted unconsciousness. Who needs marriage. Who needs fulfillment. Who needs love. Who needs Gideon. Who needs anything but sleep, sleep, sleep. . . .

The ringing of the telephone woke her in the morning. She stumbled out of bed groggily, unsure whether the call was for this or for some other number. It was a party line, and after all these years she couldn't remember whether Aunt Edwina's ring was long-long or long-short or short-long or some other combination altogether.

The telephone was situated in the bedroom Aunt Edwina used, which was along the hall next to the kitchen. Those two rooms and the bathroom, Lacey had noted the previous day, were the only relatively clean areas in the cottage, probably because they were the only rooms in regular use.

When she picked up the phone, there were already voices on the line. She was about to disconnect when she heard Gideon say, "Lacey, it's for you. You are there, aren't you?"

Her tongue was thick, still furred with the dust of the previous night's cleaning binge. "Gideon?" she asked stupidly. At first she thought it was he who was calling her, and that someone else had picked up by mistake.

And then another voice came on the line. It was a nurse from the hospital, the same one Lacey had spoken to the previous day. She had promised to phone if there was any change in Aunt Edwina's condition. Lacey realized that Gideon's phone at the bunkhouse must be merely an extension of the main phone in the cottage.

"Miss Wynward? This is Gladdie Brenner, you know, the nurse. Now before you start worrying, I'll tell you this isn't bad news. No, there hasn't been too much change in your aunt's condition. I'm phoning, actually, because she's been asking for you. She's been a little more coherent this morning . . . she was quite upset when she heard you'd been here yesterday. She was sorry she hadn't been aware of it. She said she wanted to talk to you. In fact, she begged me to ask you to come in as soon as possible, and she wouldn't settle down until I promised to do that right away. She seemed to feel it was important. She mentioned something about—"

Among the various thoughts that had poked through Lacey's tired brain was the realization that Gideon hadn't hung up. "Excuse me a moment, Miss Brenner," she interrupted. "I think someone's listening in on the extension. Would you hang up, please, Gideon?"

She heard the click of a phone being put down. "Something about what?" she asked, stifling a moment of annoyance that he would listen in so blatantly on Aunt Edwina's line.

"Well, it was a little vague. But she said it was something she ought to speak to you about at once. I can tell you this much, though. It's to do with that island property she loves so much. Actually, she may have just been having dreams of glory, because she rambled on about how she was arranging to have an elevator installed to bring her up from the boat, and how all the furniture was going to be recovered and the antiques restored."

"Aunt Edwina couldn't afford that," Lacey said numbly, hoping against hope that there had been no more Wynward charge accounts opened on the prospect of future payment by herself. "What else did she say?"

"There was something about how she was going to go back to having properly trained servants in the bunkhouse and a proper boatman for the boats. She also went on about how she'd be able to have her friends in for tea parties again and take them for grand champagne rides in the Ditchburn, just as she used to, once the refinishing was completed and the new canvas top had been made. You know how old people are. It was rather sad, really, for even if she *could* afford all those things I'm sure nearly all of her old friends are dead and gone. That's about all I was able to get out of her. She does drift in and out, you know, and she's not always rational."

So it was just rambling, Lacey decided. The nurse probably thought Aunt Edwina was potty but was too polite to say so. It was sad, touching, and terribly pathetic that an old, old woman who had lived through all the century and seen all of its marvels, all of its inventions, all of its changes in manners and mores, still clung to those lost, useless dreams of another, grander era, an era of garden parties and lace parasols. But perhaps those dreams had held Aunt Edwina together for all these years, when the swift march of events in the modern world must have been terribly confusing to her. And in truth, her pretentious little fantasies harmed no one.

Lacey promised to come to the hospital as soon as possible. "I should be able to make it by eleven o'clock or so," she said. "Will visiting hours have started by then?"

The nurse laughed. "You'd have to be mighty quick to get here by eleven," she said. "It's past that already."

Lacey had not realized it was so late. She had removed her watch for the cleaning-up the previous evening and had not restored it to her wrist. Her sleep must have been more leaden than she knew.

"Anyway," the nurse went on, "don't worry too much if you don't get here right away. Late this afternoon might be better, perhaps? She's just been given a sedative, and she's settled down very well. I don't think she'd be able to talk coherently, even if you did come. But I promised to call, so I called."

When Lacey finished the conversation with the nurse, she was still a little groggy, but ready for the prospect of a hot bath and even hotter coffee. And in that order, she decided. She still felt filthy from her efforts of the previous evening.

She slipped into the kitchen and put a pot of coffee on the hob to percolate. Then, yawning, with her fingers already loosening the front fastening of her brassiere, she headed for the bathroom. It was opposite the bedroom she had used, at the far end of the long dark hall, just around the corner from the living room. She was slipping the brassiere off her shoulders, about to enter the bathroom, when she saw the long, indolent figure tilted against the door frame of her own bedroom, watching her.

Riveted into stillness at once, she fingered the loosened brassiere in an attempt to hold it against her breasts. "Gideon," she whispered. She felt frozen. She added numbly, "I didn't expect you to be here."

"And I didn't expect to find you in a state of undress," he said in a dry tone. His cool eyes made no secret of the fact that they were appraising her scanty attire. "Please, don't bother running. I've seen bathing suits that are almost as indecent. And, if you remember, I've seen even more a time or two in my life. Have you forgotten we once went for a skinny dip together?"

She was utterly conscious of her long naked legs, of the suggestive shadows that must be visible through her thin nylon briefs, of the fact that only her nervous fingers on the unhooked brassiere kept her breasts from being exposed altogether. And to reach the clothes in her bedroom, she would have to pass Gideon. "Please go," she requested jerkily.

Lacey felt long quivers of peculiar sensation assailing her limbs as his dark, curiously speculative gaze trickled downward over her slim curves. She wanted to scream at him, *Don't look*. But the very fact of his slow appraisal seemed to have paralyzed her throat and her feet. All she could do was stare at him speechlessly, licking her dry lips, willing him to turn his eyes away.

Gideon talked calmly, as if running into a near-naked woman were the most natural thing in the world. "I certainly won't go. Your aunt gave me the run of this house many years ago, and I didn't arrive with any ulterior purpose in mind. I'm here because I sensed a certain urgency in that phone call. What is it your aunt Edwina wants to talk to you about?"

With difficulty she regained her voice, although she still felt rooted to the floor. "Nothing. She . . . she's been having fantasies, that's all. You shouldn't have been listening in."

"That phone, as it happens, is mine. And the extension is mine too. I pay for them. Why shouldn't I listen? I have a certain interest in your aunt's welfare—more, I shouldn't wonder, than you do. Now don't ask me to leave again, for I came to offer to take you to the hospital. Throw some clothes on, then we'll have a bite and go."

Lacey swallowed. "The nurse said not to hurry. Anyway, I'm about to take a bath," she said, edging toward that door instead of her own.

"Fine. I'll have a bite of food while you do," he retorted coolly. "And is that coffee I smell? I could use a decent cup."

"Gideon, no . . ." She backed into the bathroom, with visions of large towels, bolted locks, and safety. She managed to half hide herself behind the still-open door. "The coffee's not ready, because I just put it on. It won't be ready for ages. And I can get myself to the hospital, thanks."

A dark eyebrow shot up. "You think so? And which of those vintage boats do you plan to use? You're not accustomed to running them, Lacey, and they're both badly in need of a total overhaul. I think it's safer if I take you in today. I'm in no hurry." His tone turned sarcastic. "I live a life of indolence, remember? I'll hang around till you're ready. By the way, there's no bolt on that bathroom door. I removed it after your aunt locked herself in last month and didn't have the strength to push the bolt open again. But don't worry, I'm not about to follow you in. I'm not exactly starved for the sight of a fully naked female. Our next-door neighbors on the lake have a sauna where I see several, nearly every day. Usually it's disappointingly unerotic."

Lacey wet her lips again. Talk of missing bolts distressed her, and she could think of nothing to say. She was wishing she had decided to seek safety in some other room. Behind the concealment of the bathroom door she hesitated, hidden now, but with eyes locked to Gideon's while she debated her course of action. Her brain wasn't working very well.

Suddenly Gideon smiled, the warm, devastating smile she remembered from years before. And yet it was not quite the same, for his eyes remained dark, smoldering, secretive, fastened meaningly on hers. "Half-naked females," he murmured unsettlingly, "are quite another matter. And half-closed doors can be very stimulating to the imagination too." He added in a low, smoky voice, "You're a very beautiful woman, Lacey. Even more beautiful than you were as a girl, and I wouldn't have thought that was possible. Somehow I don't think you'd be a disappointment in a sauna. I hope I have a chance to find out."

Lacey pushed the door closed and leaned against it. Her heart was hammering and her eyes were closed in anguish. Her knees trembled and her palms were clammy. The after-image of Gideon's knowing smile and lithe, loose-limbed body seemed to cling to her inner eyelids. And his suggestive words spun and spiraled through her brain. She thought of him in a dim, steamy sauna, naked, with clean perspiration glistening and pouring over his bared, bronzed body. She thought of the taut, tanned skin of strong shoulders, the pale polish of hard, powerful flanks, the dusky secrets of body hair slicked with sweat or beaded with moisture. She thought of the furnace heat of his flesh.

She thought of a naked woman in that dim, steamy space beside him, and unwillingly she visualized herself.

In a fury of self-hatred she jerked on the taps of the huge old claw-footed tub, and water began to choke through the ancient plumbing system. Soon steam rose and the tub filled, the faint amber discoloration due not to lack of cleanliness, she knew, but to the iron content of the lake water.

There was a painted bentwood chair in the bathroom, and she jammed it into place beneath the door handle. After the nuances in Gideon's last remark, she didn't know whether to trust him or not. But . . . oh, God . . . the worst was, she didn't trust herself.

Gideon was thoughtful as he left Lacey behind the closed bathroom door. He walked to the kitchen, his thumbs hooked into the waistband of his close-cut black jeans.

The coffee wasn't ready, and he decided to scramble some eggs while he waited. He hadn't eaten yet, and the supplies in the fridge and in the cupboards were really his. This summer he had taken to sharing meals with old Miss Wynward in the main cottage. He had stocked no groceries at the bunkhouse—which he still referred to as the bunkhouse even though he'd renovated its interior so that it was really more of a studio.

He knew his way around the Wynward cottage. Old Miss Wynward, who had been remarkably spry until her eighty-eighth year, had finally succumbed to the natural rhythms of aging in her eighty-ninth. Her eyesight had failed badly; her arthritic old bones had lost their elasticity and their strength; her blue-veined fingers trembled so much that she could hardly lift a bone china teacup. Preservation of appearances had become something that was only in her mind, for she could no longer clean for herself, cook for herself, or care for herself in even the simplest ways. This summer Gideon had had to do those things for her. He had also had to pay most of her expenses out of his own pocket. Although her mind was sometimes clear, it was also given to lapses. In one of her more vaporous fits she had spent a pleasant afternoon in June dropping precious dollar bills into the water down at the dock, and watching in a daze of happy contentment while the slow lake waves lapped them away and then sucked them beneath the surface. By the time Gideon found her, most of a month's pension was gone.

At the beginning of the summer he had realized she shouldn't have considered coming to the island; she had simply grown too old for it. But she'd given up her room in town, as she always did at the start of each season in order to save money. The room was always then rented out, at quadruple the price, to summer tourists. Miss Wynward couldn't possibly go there; nor was there room for her in the old-age homes nearby. She shouldn't have been on the island at all, but as far as Gideon could see, there was no other option. And so he had fallen into the role of caring for her. Over the course of many summers he'd developed an affection for ancient Miss Wynward, and also an amused tolerance for her insistence on outdated standards she couldn't possibly live up to. There was something pathetically touching about her pretensions.

He was a little impatient and resentful at having to play nursemaid to an old lady, but he felt a great deal of pity for her and could see no other choice. He couldn't simply abandon her, as her family had apparently done.

It was not because of old Miss Wynward that he had returned to the Eyrie year after year, nor was it because of any ridiculous pining for Lacey Wynward. There were other reasons for his attachment to the island. For one thing, he'd always had the notion that if he were around at the right time, he might be able to acquire the property if it ever changed hands. As he didn't want to compete with the kind of money that might be offered by developers, he knew he would have to be on the spot, able to act quickly before someone started figuring out how many parcels of lake frontage could be hacked out of ten beautifully treed acres. He was genuinely attached to the island and the crumbling old cottage. It reminded him of the burned-down summer home where he'd spent so many holidays in his youth. And the Eyrie's bunkhouse, high on a point hidden by trees, did good things for his creative juices. He liked writing there, just as he liked writing in his winter cabin in the Poconos.

But for the moment, as he stirred the beaten eggs into melted butter, he wasn't thinking about his compulsion to acquire the land. Nor was he thinking about old Miss Wynward; nor about the renovations he would throw himself into once the land was his; nor about the novel he was presently engaged in writing. His mind was occupied with neither past nor future, but only with the present.

He was thinking about Lacey Wynward, naked in an old bathtub. He didn't much like the woman herself, or what she stood for. That part, the caring for her, had disintegrated long ago. But the wanting, he realized, hadn't. He could not remember desiring a woman so much in his life, at least not since that autumn of teasing and torment and first-love touching so many years before, when his desire had been worked to a fever pitch.

After a long night of restless tossing and turning, when he had been hard-pressed not to walk down through the dark path to the main cottage, Gideon had had to admit to himself that she had never been completely out of his system. She was like a sliver that had been festering for years. A thorn in his pride, perhaps? She was the only woman to whom he had ever offered marriage, and although the circumstances had not been ideal, the offer hadn't been made lightly—although he wouldn't want to admit that to Lacey now. It had been a tremendous blow to his youthful ego when she had cared more for money and social position than she had cared for him.

If he had wondered about her experience with men the previous day, he wasn't wondering now. She'd been damn near indecent in the hall, and yet she hadn't run for cover with maidenly modesty. Oh, there had been a hand held high at the brassiere fastening, although it hadn't concealed much. Through the lace of that thin garment he'd seen the ripe push of her swelling breasts, the rise and fall of her chest, the dark, well-delineated outline of thrusting nipples. Through the scanty briefs he'd seen the delicate tracery of hipbones, the haunting triangular shadow of her womanhood. She must have known she was less than decently clad, and yet she had simply stood there and stared up at him, licking her lips. She had been surprised, yes; but he felt she had also wanted to arouse him. Perhaps she was not even aware of that herself— but Gideon was aware. He knew and understood the various vibrations women sent off, and Lacey Wynward had been sending vibrations of a certain, unmistakable kind. Mating vibrations. He had felt them in the air. And that was why he had allowed the smoldering edge of sensuality to enter his voice.

Gideon imagined she was already willing, on the instinctive, subconscious level at least. As to the conscious level . . . perhaps he wouldn't allow her to do too much thinking. Perhaps he'd simply seize his opportunities. Or even better, create them. Not by entering through an unbolted door while she was bathing, though; that was a little too obvious.

He wanted to have her, and he had a deep compulsion to make the attempt—a compulsion born, perhaps, of the unnatural swiftness and suddenness with which that autumn romance had been interrupted. Would he have had this strong feeling of unfinished business between them if their love-making had culminated for him in the normal way?

As it was, he was drawn by a powerful desire to complete what had not been truly completed before. Gideon had always thought of himself as a scrupulous person, but now he wasn't so sure. Chalk it up to old pride, old passions, old hurts, or old resentments—but the truth was he didn't feel very scrupulous as far as Lacey Wynward was concerned. He didn't want her permanently. Just long enough to work her out of his system.

Chapter Three

$\mathcal{B}$y the time Lacey had finished her bath, the tantalizing aroma of bacon, eggs, toast, and coffee permeated the cottage. Somewhat to her surprise, a healthy surge of appetite quickly overcame the qualms she had about facing Gideon again. After the long labor of the previous evening, when she had stopped only for a quick sandwich, she was in need of solid sustenance.

Hearing her leave the bathroom, he called out an invitation to share the late breakfast he had made. To her relief, he didn't appear in the hall. "I'll be there in a minute," she called out, then hurried into her bedroom bundled in two large Turkish towels that covered absolutely everything. The bolt on her bedroom door was sound, and she used it.

She had accepted the offer of breakfast, but she had decided that she would not accept his offer to take her into town. The less she saw of Gideon, the better.

Sounds of a boat arriving at the dock piqued her curiosity, especially as it was followed by a female "Halloo!"

Lacey's window overlooked the lake. Hurriedly, she pulled on a cotton T-shirt. With her upper half decent, she threw open the window and leaned out. Her hair was still wet and straggly, dripping over her shoulders.

"Hi," said a shapely blonde from the dock below. She had heard the sounds at the window and looked up. "You're Lacey Wynward, aren't you?"

"Yes, I am," Lacey acknowledged. "What can I do for you?"

"Actually, I came to invite you to a party. We saw you arrive yesterday. I'd have been over then, but I thought you might like time to settle in."

Lacey wasn't surprised. People on the lakes were often remarkably friendly, especially when they occupied adjacent property. Summer acquaintances were casual, easily made, usually enjoyable.

"Perhaps you'd better tell me more about it," Laccy said with a warm smile.

"First I'd better introduce myself," said the visitor. "I'm Debbie Halloran, your nearest neighbor." She stood on the dock, holding the painter line of a racy ski boat while she talked. She was a year or so younger than Lacey, with a merry, dimpled face and a nice grin. Berry-brown from sunbathing, she was clad in the skimpiest of shorts and halter tops, with the sort of figure that didn't look as though it would be a disappointment in a sauna. Lacey had to wonder if that was the kind of party the blonde was talking about.

"To be more precise," Debbie went on, "all of us Hallorans are your nearest neighbors. My brother, his wife, their kids, various cousins and uncles and aunts—you'll meet the whole gang later. Our island is the one just to the north, within waving distance of Gideon's bunkhouse. We're having a barbecue tonight. Actually, it's a sort of get-together for all the islanders in the Wynward group. An island-warming, we call it. It's an annual July thing, to get the season off to a good start. Well, at least it's been annual every year since we built, and that was about five years ago. You absolutely have to come! Everyone's dying to meet you."

Lacey guessed that Gideon would probably be there, along with everyone else. But with cousins and uncles and aunts and kids and assorted neighbors invited, it didn't sound like the kind of thing she needed to avoid. She wasn't much in the mood for partying, but to turn down the invitation would be an insult, an advertisement to everyone within hailing distance that she intended to hold herself aloof.

"I'd love to come," she said. "What time?"

"Great! We'll be starting at six thirty or so. Well, actually, any time that suits you . . ." Debbie Halloran's eyes turned in a new direction and widened with faint surprise. "Gideon! What are you doing over here? I thought this was your writing time of day."

Lacey could see his advance on the dock directly below her—the top of a dark head, the breadth of shoulder, the flattened fingertips thrust casually into the hip pocket of his lean black jeans. He didn't look up at the window. "I came over to ask the young Miss Wynward about the old Miss Wynward," he said, his voice easy. He came to a halt near Debbie Halloran. Lacey could not see his face.

Debbie was smiling, her head tilted flirtatiously to one side. To Lacey it seemed obvious that the girl had a thing for Gideon. "I'm expecting you tonight, Gideon. Any chance you could take me kite-skiing this afternoon, just to get started on the season's fun?" she asked. "We have to christen my new ski boat. I've been looking forward to it all winter."

"I've agreed to take Lacey in to the hospital."

Debbie's face fell.

"That's not necessary, Gideon," Lacey inserted, drawing his attention upward. She felt self-conscious about the hideous, dripping tangle of her hair, but she made no effort to hide it. It was better if Gideon saw her looking unattractive. "Really, I'd rather go by myself. And I have other errands in town—a load of laundry, for one thing. Besides, Aunt Edwina is under sedation. In spite of that call, the nurse said she probably wouldn't be able to talk to me today."

Gideon was frowning as he looked up at the window. "Still, it's best if I take you. Those old boats of yours aren't too reliable."

"I used to manage them perfectly well, and I'm sure I still can. If I can't get one of them going, I'll call the marina to pick me up." She paused and added, "Frankly, Gideon, I'm not particularly keen on having company today. I've arranged to meet a man."

Gideon studied her for a moment, his eyes enigmatic. At last he shrugged indifferently. "As you wish," he said at last and then turned back to Debbie Halloran, who was smiling expectantly. Perhaps she was pleased to think that Lacey, who had made no effort to hide her mussed-up hair, and who had the prospect of another man in the offing, wasn't about to become a rival.

"Well, Gideon? How about it?"

"Glad to, Deb. An afternoon of water sport sounds like just what the doctor ordered. Two o'clock?"

"No, twelve thirty," Debbie said promptly, eyes sparkling. "First I'm going to feed you a hamburger. Big, plump, juicy, and medium rare, with all those special Gideon Jerrold trimmings. I haven't forgotten any of them since last summer. Fresh onion bun, lettuce, bread and butter pickles, homemade chili sauce—"

Feeling as if she were intruding, Lacey decided it was time to withdraw. "Thanks a lot for your invitation, Debbie," she interrupted. "I'll see you tonight."

But after she had closed the window, she spent long enough adjusting the curtain to see the light kiss Gideon bestowed on Debbie Halloran's cheek. She saw the way Debbie returned it more lingeringly, tiptoeing up to whisper in his ear. At the same time her fingers trailed over Gideon's hip in an unmistakably intimate way.

It looked as though the two were very familiar with each other. Lacey had to wonder how often Debbie Halloran had visited the bunkhouse over the course of the past few years. No more than fifty yards separated the two islands at the north end—

and some summer acquaintances could become very, very friendly indeed.

Lacey finished dressing thoughtfully while a conflict of emotions played tug-of-war inside her. Gideon's brief and disconcerting attentions in the hall were not so extraordinary, considering the state of dishabille she had been in at the time. He'd never follow through, not with another woman, a willing one, close at hand. Lacey knew she should be glad, glad, glad . . .

She decided she ought to encourage the relationship.

"Debbie's very pretty," she observed artlessly a short time later in the kitchen. Her hair was still wet, if respectably combed. "Is she one of the reasons you haven't felt the need of marriage, Gideon?"

He gave her a bland, uncommunicative look. "She's a good friend. I've known her for several years."

"Is she the last in your long string of summer romances?"

Lacey hadn't intended the observation to sound so shrewish. Gideon's fork paused in the act of spearing a rasher of bacon. "That's a loaded remark."

Lacey sighed. "Not loaded, just realistic. I'm sorry if it sounded judgmental, for I really don't care what romances you've had."

"It was the word 'summer' I objected to, actually. It sounds so damn frivolous, as though I change women with the seasons."

"Don't you? As I recall, you used to. One for the summer, one for the autumn . . ."

"What on earth are you talking about?"

"You're not going to pretend I was your very first love, are you, Gideon? Now that we're adults, we can be honest. You weren't exactly inexperienced eight years ago. I remember the bubbly little blonde you were sleeping with earlier that summer."

"Who gave you that idea?"

"Aunt Edwina."

When he stared at her, his face expressionless, she added with a forced smile, "Oh, don't worry, Gideon. It didn't have a single thing to do with my vanishing act—although it did help to bring me to my senses. It was a quick cure for a silly summer infatuation, that's all. As soon as I saw you without blinkers, I knew Aunt Edwina was right. You weren't the man for me. Effervescent blondes are more your type." Lacey was sure her smile had just the right touch of sophisticated indifference. "I approve of Debbie; she seems very nice. How long have you been involved with her?"

"That," he drawled, "is none of your damn business."

She manufactured a light laugh. "Yes, I agree with you; it isn't. Whatever you do with your summer friend is of no particular interest to me. So to set your mind at rest, Gideon, Debbie's welcome on my island any time you want to entertain her in your own quarters. Any time at all. Believe me, I won't be walking up to the bunkhouse for any reason whatsoever."

She waited while he digested that, then asked casually, "Do you always do your cooking in Aunt Edwina's kitchen?"

"This year . . . yes. My supplies are stored here."

"I'm truly grateful for the breakfast. But is there something wrong with the cooking facilities up at the bunkhouse?"

"Is that a delicate way of telling me to use my own kitchen from now on?"

Lacey gave him a calm smile. "Yes. And if you could clean out your supplies . . . not that I really mind them cluttering up the fridge, Gideon, but I should hate to touch anything of yours by mistake."

"Fine," Gideon returned with absolute calmness. "I'll do it later this afternoon, if that's soon enough."

So far, so good, thought Lacey. Between separate mealtimes and permission to carry on to his heart's content up at the bunkhouse, Gideon wasn't likely to be too much of a threat.

"Who's this man you're meeting?"

Lacey met his eyes coolly. It was a local real estate agent with whom she had corresponded off and on over the years, but she was only too happy if Gideon got the wrong impression. "That," she said, "is none of your damn business."

Gideon laughed and rose to his feet. "Touché," he acknowledged as he carried his plate to the sink.

"Leave the dishes to me," Lacey suggested. "I'm about to dive into some more cleaning anyway; I have a couple of hours to spare before I head off for the hospital." She glanced pointedly at her watch. "Now if you'll excuse me . . ."

Gideon took the hint. With a wry salute, he aimed toward the door. "See you," he said indifferently, and Lacey watched as his long, lean frame ambled out the door.

The irrational half of her desperately wanted to

call him back. Fortunately the rational half was in control.

Starting the ancient Ditchburn was a great deal more difficult than it had been eight years before. And when the engine finally caught, the water pump that was supposed to cool the engine still wasn't spewing water out the rear of the big antique boat. It took Lacey nearly half an hour to get it going properly, but get it going she did. At least it was better than the old Dippy, whose engine didn't even kick over.

The thirty-foot mahogany launch was difficult to maneuver, too, and it stalled twice en route to the public docks in the tiny town of Hubbard's Landing, where Lacey had left her car. She considered taking the boat directly in to the marina, but decided against that course. Taking it in was easy enough, but getting it out might cost several hundred dollars—or more. Lacey didn't think she could swing it, not when she was still waiting for the bad news about Aunt Edwina's marina bill.

The washing, the appointment with the real estate agent, and the visit to the hospital fully filled the afternoon. The last of these missions was wasted. Aunt Edwina slept through the entire stay, and the friendly nurse informed Lacey that she hadn't been too rational anyway when last awake. "She's not entirely senile yet," Gladdie Brenner said, "but her mind comes and goes, and the medications leave her confused too. Maybe she'll be better tomorrow."

"How's her heart?"

Gladdie Brenner shrugged. "Holding out. But at her age . . . I wouldn't expect too much, Miss

Wynward. She's had a long, full life. She'll be ninety come September, won't she? That's a ripe old age, in anyone's book."

Lacey finally left a note at the nursing station, to be given to her aunt during some more lucid period.

The old Ditchburn guzzled fifty dollars' worth of gas at the marine pump before it grudgingly agreed to make the return trip to the Eyrie. "You be paying up the Wynward charge, then?" Hobie Hubbard inquired when Lacey reached into her purse.

"Not today," she said firmly, "but I'll pay cash for this."

He took the money without comment, eyeing the other contents of her wallet. He didn't look pleased.

Even with the big infusion of liquid cash, the Ditchburn stalled several times on the return trip, the last of these just as Lacey was easing it into its slip. Fortunately its forward drift carried it for the final few feet.

It was past six thirty before she was ready for the Hallorans' party, and she could see no option but to go by canoe. Even if the Ditchburn started, there was unlikely to be room for it at the Hallorans' dock. Gideon's boat was still in the slip, and perhaps she could have hitched a ride with him, but she preferred not to. She wanted mobility to leave the party at her own time, with her own means of conveyance.

She took a big double-sided safety lantern for the return trip, which was only a short distance along a protected, shallow shoreline where larger boats wouldn't venture.

The canoe was pulled high on a boat ramp. It looked as though it hadn't been used for some time; cobwebs infested its interior. Three minutes after Lacey launched it, its bone-dry cedar strip hull was awash in an inch of water, and so were her feet. She wouldn't have needed directions to get to the party. Sounds of the island-warming—laughter, shouts of greeting, a blare of music—could be heard even before her canoe rounded the far tip of the Eyrie.

Her leather sandals were uncomfortably squishy as she stepped out into a gathering of strangers who didn't intend to remain strangers for very long. Within seconds a drink had been thrust in her hand. Within thirty minutes there had been thirty introductions, a good deal of jovial chatter, a few bad jokes and a few good ones. A rather drunk host had bussed her on the cheek, four people had issued vague invitations for the future, and several rounds of canapés had been passed. Children of assorted sizes darted in and out, shrieking with laughter. Liquor flowed. Everyone was having a wonderful time.

Lacey didn't see Gideon or Debbie Halloran. She didn't allow herself to speculate on where they might be; nor did she allow her gaze to dwell on the Eyrie's bunkhouse, which was visible from where she stood.

The Hallorans had a large, modern, expensive spread. Prior to the serving of the barbecue, someone gave her a tour. The architect-designed cottage was a modified A-frame, with great swoops of glass and native stone. Enormous decks and patios surrounded it on various levels; garden furniture was everywhere. A number of outbuildings were staggered through the property. Most of them were well hidden by trees—guest houses; cottages for various members of the large clan, including Debbie's personal sleeping cabin; the sauna Gideon had mentioned; a truly enormous four-slip boathouse that housed a small fortune in fiberglass, metal, and chrome. One slip was empty, and Debbie's ski boat wasn't there.

It arrived half an hour later, in the most dramatic way, just as a long buffet table was being loaded with barbecued ribs, bean salads, potato salads, and an assortment of other edibles. Suddenly everyone was looking up into the air beyond the Eyrie—and there was Debbie, high in the sky, riding a rainbow-striped kite. She landed out of sight in safe open water and several minutes later arrived at the dock still on skis, but minus the kite. Gideon dropped her off, pulled in the towline, and swerved away to return the ski boat to its niche for the night.

Lacey was down near the dock when Debbie emerged on a ladder, waterlogged but jubilant with excitement. "I did it! I finally did it! I wanted you all to see—oh, *God*, I'm so damn tired. It was hard work getting up! But Gideon's a good teacher . . . great heaven, is that *food* I smell? I could eat about a hundred and seventy-five horses, one for every one on the motor of that sweet little boat. Hi, Lacey! Glad to see you made it."

It ought to be hard not to like Debbie. Lacey wanted to, but wasn't sure she could. How could anyone look so damn appealing with hair like wet straw and a badly sunburned nose? It was disturbing for Lacey to realize she was jealous, when she had no interest in Gideon herself.

After the barbecue the children vanished as if by magic. Someone told Lacey that they'd all been taken to one of the other islands, where tents had been set up for a sleep-out, with the older teenagers in charge.

It was dark by then, with light bestowed by stars and strings of lawn lights. The music was slower, dreamier. Inside the A-frame and out on a large wooden deck, people were dancing. A few had aimed for the sauna. Lacey was on a flagstone patio, lounging on a lawn chair with a similarly indolent married couple, when Gideon appeared at her side. "Dance?" he asked.

Reluctantly, she looked up. "Where's your regular partner?"

"Gone to the sauna. I wasn't quite ready for that kind of steam."

"I'm not much of a dancer, Gideon."

"Neither am I."

"Go on, Lacey," urged the man sitting at her elbow. "If you don't accept, he's going to ask my wife. And then I'll have to spend the rest of the evening listening to lectures about what a rotten dancer I am."

"Besides," added his wife, rising to her feet, "we're about to dance too. Aren't we, Roger? Hmmm? Do me a favor, Lacey, and accept. It's the only way I'll get this old stick-in-the-mud out onto the floor."

Lacey could think of no easy out, for it was too early to make a polite departure. Gideon led her to the outdoor deck, the darker of the two dance floors. She tried to keep some distance between them, but it was hard—obviously awkward, when the pace of the music made it difficult not to dance cheek-to-cheek. Everyone else was in close tandem.

At first she tried to justify the separation by chattering nervously about anything and everything that came to mind. She recounted every word she had heard at the hospital; asked Gideon endless questions about her aunt's condition prior to the heart attack; questioned him about the kite-skiing; made inconsequential remarks about the various changes time had wrought on the lake. She told about the problems with the Dippy, the Ditchburn, and the canoe.

"I'll have a look at them," Gideon promised. "But don't expect miracles."

"I don't. But they're such wonderful old boats, I hate to—"

"Look, Lacey, I'm not going to do anything about them tonight. Now relax. This is a dance floor, not a military exercise."

"—abandon them altogether. They're museum pieces, I know, but—"

"Relax," Gideon commanded sternly, forcibly pulling her against him.

She didn't want to be in his arms, but when she was, she soon melted into them as if she belonged there. Feeling the length of him molded so closely against her, her wanton imagination took an unwanted leap back in time. . . .

They had danced once to an old hand-cranked Victrola at the Wynward cottage, supplying it with hard, thick vintage records whose scratchy quality had made them both laugh with glee. Aunt Edwina had been down the hall, but she hadn't paid much attention on that occasion, because the joyous sounds hadn't suggested anything improper. And Lacey's cumbersome ankle cast had made the dancing very inelegant, another cause for merriment.

But then there had been a slow tune, to which they had done no more than stand and sway. Lacey had deliberately pressed her young body against Gideon's, breathless with her daring, hoping for and yet fearing the natural response she'd heard others talk about. It had happened, and it had been the first time she'd ever aroused a man's desire.

A man's? No, she reminded herself. A boy's.

Gideon the full-grown man had better control over his bodily reactions, and to Lacey's relief, she felt no stirring, no quickening, no burgeoning to betray a need she didn't care to think about. She felt that her own reactions, which included an assortment of quakes and quivers, were probably more indecent than his. The feeling of his mouth against her hair and his fingers moving on her spine had the most extraordinary effect on her. She was dizzied by the heady, subtle scent of him, an erotic compound of shaving soap, earthy wood smells, and the faint trace of tobacco. The night, the mood, and the music had numbed the rational part of her mind; at this stolen moment only the irrational seemed to exist.

Several dances later Gideon murmured, "Sauna? I'm altogether ready for that kind of steam now."

She snapped away from him, jerking free of his arms. "You go ahead," she said, "and rescue your friend Debbie. I imagine she's getting more than a little hot by now, waiting for you."

Gideon had the gall to look amused. In the dim light of the deck, his sardonic grin gleamed white. He didn't follow when Lacey wheeled away quickly and left, her goal the sodden canoe.

It wasn't really safe for a nighttime trip, but she didn't feel very safe staying there, either. She paddled as if her life depended on it, and perhaps it did. By the time she reached home, the canoe's gunwales were only a few inches above the water-line.

Chapter Four

The morning brought a small but nasty surprise for Lacey. She woke early and listened for other movements in the creaky old cottage. She was relieved to hear none. She rolled out of bed, wrapped herself decently in a bathrobe with the sash tied very tight, and cautiously unlocked her bedroom door. The hall was empty. She inched out. No sounds came from the kitchen.

She splashed her face in the bathroom, making a mental note to buy a new bolt for this door on her next trip to town. In the meantime, she decided, all bathing would be done in the lake, in a swimsuit.

She made for the kitchen with visions of freshly percolated coffee beginning to bubble in her head. Still half asleep, she filled the pot with water and turned on the stove, then groped for the coffee tin she had placed on a cupboard shelf the day before. Her fingers connected with air.

She opened the cupboard door more fully. Nothing was there. No coffee tin, no instant coffee, no jam jars, no boxes of cereal, no tin cans. Perhaps she had picked the wrong cupboard? Were the supplies somewhere else? Not in the next cupboard, certainly, she discovered at once. She flew around the kitchen, opening doors, growing more frantic as she found nothing but china plates, tumblers, mixing bowls, pots and pans, and various other inedibles.

And then she tried the fridge. It was empty, but for a few ice cubes in the freezer. The supplies were gone—all of them. They must have been removed sometime yesterday afternoon, while she was at the hospital. Perhaps Debbie Halloran had helped Gideon with the task. Anger at him rent the air as Lacey uttered an audible and not very ladylike curse. Damn him for not telling her that *all* the supplies were his!

Her anger became a slow simmer when she realized he must have been feeding Aunt Edwina. She remembered now that, during their conversation on the dance floor the previous evening, he had told her of her aunt's helplessness throughout the early days at the cottage. In late May and throughout the month of June, Gideon had informed her, Aunt Edwina had been unable to care for herself. Lacey supposed she owed him an enormous debt of gratitude for that.

All the same . . . it was a bit much for him to clean out the kitchen completely, with no advance warning. Did he expect that she'd go crawling to him for food? She certainly wouldn't.

Annoyance had awakened her completely, giving focus to her actions. She dressed quickly, in slim slacks and a full-sleeved peasant blouse suitable for a quick trip to town.

But today she and the balky old Ditchburn simply couldn't come to terms. After half an hour of trying, she gave up. The Dippy was no better. And the canoe, although it might have improved a little with the dried wood now damp and beginning to swell, a process which would tend to fill in the leaky chinks, wasn't up to such a long trip.

Gideon's jaunty orange boat, looking so damn mechanically perfect and watertight as it swayed against its moorings, added insult to injury. It had the effect of a smug I-told-you-so smile. Lacey swore to herself that she'd never, never ask him for help.

Hobie Hubbard's wife answered the marina phone. "It's an emergency," Lacey said, explaining only as much as was necessary.

"Hobie's in the workshop right now. I'm sure he'll get around to it as soon as possible. By the way, Miss Wynward, how soon were you planning to settle your aunt's bill?"

Lacey recognized tactful pressure when she heard it. "How much is it?"

Mrs. Hubbard mentioned a figure that caused a disbelieving gasp on Lacey's end of the phone. "It's been adding up for years," Hobie's wife explained. "We didn't like to cut old Miss Wynward's credit off, when we've had Wynwards for customers since the year one."

"I . . . er . . . forgot to bring my checkbook north with me."

"Cash would do."

Lacey remembered the several fifty-dollar bills that Hobie had spotted on the previous day. But she needed that money for groceries and other day-to-day expenses; she couldn't exist on air. "I'll have to make a trip to the bank, Mrs. Hubbard, and arrange to have some money transferred. Can you wait for a few days?"

"Certainly," came the bland answer. There was a short pause. "Well, Miss Wynward, I'll give Hobie your message."

"When do you think he can come?"

"He's kind of busy for the next little while, but . . . well, I'll mention it to him. Perhaps he'll manage to get there sometime."

Lacey cooled off by changing into a bathing suit and going for a furious swim.

By noon, three hours later, Hobie still hadn't put in an appearance. By that time the ice water Lacey was drinking only had the effect of reminding her of the gnawing hole in her stomach. A second call to the marina produced the smooth assurance that Hobie would be along as soon as he was free, but by now Lacey had gotten the general idea. Until she promised to hand over all her cash, he wasn't about to arrive.

She might have asked the Hallorans for help, but as she'd only met them the previous day, that was just as hard as asking Gideon. Finally she swallowed her pride and took the path to the bunkhouse.

The bunkhouse was really like another cottage, a large single-storied one, but very simple, with a screened porch and a warren of tiny bedrooms inside. It had been built about ninety years before to house the armies of household servants who used to accompany the Wynwards during their annual northern migrations. Till well after the turn of the century, Lacey knew, they had transported everyone and everything: cook, butler, maids, undermaids, bags, baggage, steamer trunks, crates full of blankets and supplies, even mahogany chests full of the family silver. It was the railways that had made Muskoka fashionable for the rich from certain parts of the States: it was on a direct line, in an era when there were few cars and no highway connections to closer resorts. The trip had taken at least two days, sometimes three. The whole entourage would travel north as far as Gravenhurst by rail, then detrain and make the rest of the voyage on water, by steamer boat. Several huge steamers had plied the Muskoka lakes in those days, stopping at docks and wharfs, doing errands of all sorts, even filling short shopping lists and delivering the morning milk in old-fashioned, bulge-necked bottles.

As she spotted the bunkhouse through the trees, Lacey was a little surprised to see that its trim had been painted and the dark stain on the frame structure freshly applied. It was in far better condition than the main cottage. There was a new roof, too, and neat new screens on the porch. Gideon's work, she supposed.

She knocked at the porch door. He called out an acknowledgment, but didn't arrive immediately. She began to think about Debbie Halloran, about the sauna the previous evening, about the small gap between this island and the next, about two people entwined in bed. . . .

But when Gideon arrived at the screen door, he was fully dressed, wearing cut-off jeans and a faded denim-blue shirt rolled up at the sleeves. He hadn't shaved. He was standing at a greater height than she, for the porch was raised by several steps. Lacey kept her eyes on his face, a safer view than his long, muscular legs. His feet were bare, too, and the intimacy of those naked toes bothered her unnaturally.

"Sorry," he apologized. "I was in the middle of a paragraph."

"You were writing? Oh . . ."

"I do, you know," he said dryly. He studied Lacey coolly from on high, a slow assessing look that measured her from top to toe. She suddenly felt overly conscious of the scoop neck of the peasant blouse which, while quite decent, did reveal just the faintest beginning of her breasts. She fingered the front of it in an uncharacteristically nervous gesture.

Gideon didn't open the screen door or invite her in; instead he glanced at his watch. "So late? I ought to have stopped writing before now. My working day usually ends at noon—a lazy fellow like me doesn't like to overdo the exertion." He grinned derisively to emphasize his sarcasm. "Well, Lacey, what can I do for you?"

"When are you next going into town? I wouldn't mind a lift. I can't get any of the boats going."

"Off to visit your aunt?"

"Well, yes, I do have to do that. And visit the bank. And shop for groceries."

"Mmm," he said thoughtfully, rubbing the rakish texture of his jaw. His face was absolutely innocent. "Sounds like a long trip, what with the drive to the hospital. Meeting any gentlemen today?"

She exercised patience. "As it happens, no."

"Then I might be able to manage it. Come in,

won't you, while I get shaven, shorn, and dressed for the day?"

"I can wait for you at the other cottage. Just shout when you're ready."

He shrugged, his eyes glinting with golden mockery. "As you wish. But you might be interested to know that there's a pot of coffee on the stove and some pancake batter in a bowl. The sausages are a little cold, seeing as I cooked them for you a full four hours ago. You'll have to warm them up. But it's all there, if you don't mind looking after yourself."

"You knew I'd be over," she accused. "Damn you, Gideon."

"I didn't *know*. I guessed. I had a look at the Ditchburn last night after I came in. I think I can get it back to working condition for you, with some small adjustments—but not today. I have plans for the afternoon." He opened the door and stepped aside while she mounted the steps, drawn by hunger.

"Plans?"

He tilted a dark brow. "To visit your aunt, of course. You don't think I'd offer to tie up a nice sunny day like this, do you, if my plans didn't coincide with yours?"

As they entered the main body of the cottage, Lacey was stunned to see that the old, dark interior had been totally changed. All the myriad partitions had been ripped out, turning most of the area into one enormous room. Large, new picture windows overlooked the east and the west, views that didn't take in the Hallorans' cottage, but did include several other islands in the Wynward group. In early morning and late afternoon, Lacey imagined, the windows would be pleasantly bright, with sun filtering through the tall-shady trees. The furniture in the room was very simple and included a huge refinished pine table that obviously served as a desk. It was littered with paper and flanked by a typing table.

"I like space for thinking," Gideon explained. "I suppose I should have gotten your permission. Perhaps you'll forgive me, as it's really an improvement to your property."

"It's about a thousand percent better," Lacey said enthusiastically, but then she remembered that she mustn't allow herself to establish that kind of warm rapport with Gideon. With an effort, she pulled back into her protective shell.

The only small rooms now in existence were the kitchen, the bathroom, and the one tiny bedroom. all located along the same side of the cottage. Lacey made her way into the first of these while Gideon vanished into the last. As she helped herself to a very welcome repast, she could hear sounds of a banging closet door, a shower, an electric razor. She tried not to let visual images intrude, but in her mind she kept seeing his strong unshaven jaw and his powerfully muscled calves, as she had seen them when he stood above her on the porch.

She'd eaten her fill and washed her plate when he reappeared, clad in cool putty-colored linen slacks and a short-sleeved Madras shirt in a soft, faded pastel plaid. To Lacey's eyes, he looked unbearably handsome in his town attire. With an ache of longing, she turned her gaze away.

"I may as well polish off your leftovers," Gideon decided, helping himself to the few sausages that remained in the pan. "It may be breakfast for you, but it's lunch for me. Can you hang on for a few minutes?"

"If you'll excuse me, I have to get changed too. Shall I meet you down at the boathouse?"

"Sure. Fifteen minutes? I have a few things to do. I'll shout when I get there."

"You won't have to," Lacey said. "I'll hear you."

She thought she would hear him with every single one of her nerve endings, even if he was as silent as a cat.

Lacey had already purchased her groceries, top priority on her mind, when she realized it would do the perishables no good to sit for a long time in a hot, stuffy car or out in a sunny open boat. And sit they would have to, for the hospital was in the town of Bracebridge, a full half-hour's drive from the tiny settlement of Hubbard's Landing.

Therefore, at Gideon's suggestion, the afternoon's expedition changed into two trips. He loaded the groceries into the boat while Lacey made a quick foray into the bank, arranging to transfer cash from her account in the States. The manager, helpful though he was, told her it would probably take about a week. He also mentioned to Lacey that her aunt's account was overdrawn. "I know I shouldn't have allowed it," he said with a frown. "But as she *is* a Wynward . . ."

"I'll look after it," Lacey said as steadily as possible, wondering how many more nasty surprises awaited her.

With Gideon's help, it took only a short while to return to the Eyrie and get the produce and dairy

products put away. And then they were on their
way again.

The visit to the hospital was poignant and not
particularly productive. As to her physical state,
Aunt Edwina was no better, no worse. Her ancient
face was a seamed map that showed the furrows of
great age and the drastically deteriorated state of
her health, but even near death it was possible to
see that she had once been a handsome, patrician
woman. Her mind wandered too much for any
meaningful conversation to be held.

She didn't appear to recognize Lacey at all, but
when she saw Gideon, some tiny spark entered her
rheumy, dulled old eyes. Her mind was in the past.

"Will you order the champagne for me, Gideon?" Her voice was a quavery echo of what it once
had been. "Not domestic, please. And make sure
it's vintage. My brother likes Brut '28 . . . or is it
'29? Oh dear, so confusing . . . get thirty cases,
please. Put it on my charge, and tell that man . . .
tell him . . . oh, dear, you can't charge that sort of
thing in Canada, can you? Well, take the money
from my purse. And don't let them fob you off with
poor quality when you buy the caviar. Order it
from New York if you have to—I have a charge at
Delmonico's. Or is it . . . is it . . . ? Oh, dear, I
can't remember . . . perhaps I'd better call and see
if Delmonico's is still in business. The world changes so fast . . ."

Lacey could only listen, feeling an ache of empa-
thy for a dying old woman whose world had died
half a century before her.

"I think I'll wear my big floppy picture hat . . .
the pink one . . . I bought it in Paris but I've never
worn it . . . and I'll have to have a new dress

designed by Worth. Of course I'll wear the jewels for an occasion like this . . . or did I sell the jewels?" Her face began to crumple. "Oh, dear, I'll be so ashamed if I have no jewels. What will everyone think? And Jacob will be so angry if I sold them . . . but I don't suppose I did . . . I wouldn't do a thing like that . . . they're supposed to go to Lacey, you know . . ."

Lacey and Gideon exchanged glances. They both knew she had sold her jewels years before.

Lacey touched her aunt's hand. "It's all right, Aunt Edwina. I don't need any jewels."

But Aunt Edwina was still looking at Gideon, her purse of a mouth tremulous. "I've invited your mother," she quivered. "I've decided to forgive her, you see. And I suppose she has to be there, considering . . . even though . . . well, we can't have anyone wondering why she's not there, can we? Oh, dear, it's so confusing, so hard to make up these lists. So many people will be devastated if I don't include them . . . but the Country Club said to keep it down to five hundred . . . the tent won't hold more. I don't have time to have extra invitations engraved anyway. You'll have to arrange for boats, too, Gideon, for all the guests coming up from the States. They've taken over a whole hotel, you know, because their servants need rooms too. I've ordered two boxcars of fresh rose petals to strew on the paths. Do you think that will be enough? And shall we serve strawberries with the champagne? Or will that be too ordinary?"

Gideon didn't notice that Lacey, seated on a straight plastic-covered bedside chair, had stiffened and turned a little pale. "Strawberries would be fine," he said, "and so will the rose petals."

A contented smile drifted across the ruination of her once-fine face. Edwina Wynward closed her sunken eyes and drifted into a dreamland of her own, where all was for the best in the best of all possible worlds.

"I think she was talking about my grandfather's wedding," Lacey said quietly when they were in the car, on the first leg of the trip back to the cottage. "He was married up here in Muskoka. Aunt Edwina arranged it all."

"But she said something about my mother, who wouldn't have been around back then."

"Well, perhaps she was traveling back and forth in time. My father was married up here, too, although the wedding was far simpler."

"Oh," said Gideon.

And that was all that was said. Lacey was not anxious to discuss Aunt Edwina's meanderings, and neither was Gideon. Their reasons were different, but the end result was the same.

During the next few days, while Lacey waited for funds to be transferred from the States, the hospital visits fell into a regular pattern. Gideon seemed determined to visit Aunt Edwina as often as she did, so Lacey came to accept and expect his daily offer of marine transportation. He had restored the Ditchburn to some kind of function, but it was undependable to say the least, and she knew it was really in desperate need of Hobie Hubbard's attention. She couldn't ask for that until she paid Aunt Edwina's monumental bill, and so the daily outing with Gideon became a ritual. Usually the trips were made in the morning, with Gideon foregoing his writing. "And glad to," he had said with a sardonic grin, mocking his own antipathy to work. Lacey assumed he wanted to save his afternoons for more traditional summertime pursuits. She politely refused a few invitations to swim or water-ski and continued to throw herself into the neverending task of cottage cleanup.

If Gideon still had designs on her, he made no overt moves, and gradually she was lulled into believing that if she kept her distance, so would he. She even began to enjoy his company in a very guarded way, although she was careful not to let too much warmth creep into her manner.

Aunt Edwina's ramblings continued in much the same vein as they had during the first visit. She was obsessed with the past, and the weddings of Lacey's grandfather and father were often on her mind. But there were other hallucinations too—talk of rebuilding the cottage, of hiring vast numbers of servants, of landscaping the property and giving grand garden parties for her friends—all sad symptoms of the progressive deterioration of her mind. Her worn-out body continued to struggle for existence, and the medical reports suggested that the weak flutters of her heart had settled into a less critical pattern.

There was another small financial surprise waiting for Lacey at the local butcher shop, where she tried to order a special cut of meat one day. A yellowed old bill was pulled out of a drawer. Fortunately or unfortunately, depending on one's point of view, Aunt Edwina's credit had been cut off nearly a decade before, and she had had to start buying her meat at the supermarket, presumably ordering cheaper cuts. The butcher's bill was therefore high, but not impossible. Lacey managed to pay it with the funds she had on hand, but she made a second trip to the bank to increase the amount of the requested transfer.

At last the funds arrived, and then there was another reason for the continued acceptance of Gideon's help. The Ditchburn and the DP went in for much-needed service, and Hobie Hubbard didn't promise either of them in short order. He said he would have to hand-tool some of the parts.

During all trips to the hospital they traveled in Lacey's car. It seemed a fair exchange for the use of Gideon's boat. Besides, he hadn't offered to drive; she wasn't even sure whether he owned a car. If he did, perhaps he was ashamed of its condition. She knew he wasn't nearly as broke as he had been eight years ago—the racy orange runabout and a few other things testified to that—but his various comments had suggested that he didn't have an overload of assets. With the life he led, boats were probably of more consequence than cars.

Lacey was well entrenched in her protective shell. The cool, polite finishing-school manners she had learned in her youth were no longer her personal ideal for good breeding, but they did have their uses. It had become much easier to maintain an emotional distance from Gideon. She used such defenses as she could think of to keep his mind from becoming wayward—a lack of lipstick, hair pushed unsuggestively behind her ears, clothes that revealed as little as possible of herself. She never went swimming unless she had seen him take off in Debbie Halloran's ski boat, and her customary outfit for the trips to town was a navy blue linen slack suit that was smart without being in the least suggestive. Its boxy jacket prevented attention from being directed to any of the wrong parts of herself.

Whether because of the exterior garb or because of some other reason, to Lacey's relief Gideon was no longer paying attention to any of those wrong parts. His manner had become as cool, as impersonal, and as enigmatic as hers. His face was usually a mask.

He broke the mold one afternoon by arriving unexpectedly while Lacey was swimming. Debbie, it seemed, had dropped him off at the other end of the island. After a noncommittal greeting, he stood on the dock and watched her for a long time while she remained in the water, unwilling to step out and reveal the inadequacies of her black bikini. She was exhausted and waterlogged when he finally uttered a curt good-bye, swiveled on his heel, and left.

But she had seen the dark desire growing in his face, and the following morning it changed the mood between them. Occasionally during the drive she found her eyes drifting sideways to touch on his profile, half expecting to surprise him in the act of staring at her. Invariably his gaze was directed elsewhere—at a rolling sweep of rock-strewn grassland, at a half-fallen barn whose weathered timbers had seen better days, at a small bog of bulrushes beside the road, at a starkly beautiful rust-colored rock cut that had been blasted to accommodate the highway.

Every time, she wished she hadn't looked. Each glance imprinted some different part of him in her mind. The bend of his knees. The long, strong, tapered fingers resting loosely against his thighs. The dusting of dark hair on his tanned forearms, a contrast to the white of his short-sleeved seersucker shirt. A cord of muscle alongside his throat. The curve of his ear. The tousle of brown hair at the nape of his neck, a little too long and casual because the barber shop would probably never be high on his list of priorities.

The return drive was no better than the drive to the hospital had been, for Lacey remained fully aware of Gideon's physique with a forcefulness she had lulled herself into believing she could suppress. She still wasn't breathing easily when they reached Hubbard's Landing. Gideon spoke casually as they neared the complex of public docks where his boat was tied up. "I have news for you, Lacey. Before we set off today, I chucked some things into a cooler. How about it? After a hot trip into town, nothing like a picnic and a swim. I have the perfect spot in mind. That deserted cove where we went once years ago, it's still deserted. Well? Are you game?"

Her stomach tied into a knot of tension, and she almost swerved into one of the summer jaywalkers who continually misused the main street.

"Sorry," she said, tossing out the first excuse she could think of. "I intend to spend the afternoon taking a nap."

"Ah," Gideon said and didn't try to press her.

Within minutes they were in Gideon's boat, skimming across the lake. The speed flapped Lacey's long hair and caused Gideon's to ruffle in disarray. He looked younger, she thought, carefree and good-tempered, and despite all cautionary reminders to keep her eyes to herself, she almost forgot to watch where they were going.

"What are you doing?" she asked in sudden

alarm when she saw that their course was not taking them toward the Eyrie.

"Exactly what I told you," he replied with disconcerting coolness. "I packed the cooler in the boat hours ago, and I see no reason to change my plans. The cove is a perfect place for picnicking, swimming—and napping, too, as it happens."

"But I'd rather go back to the cottage! I still have a lot of cleaning to do!"

The lazy white grin spread over his face. "The work can wait. Don't you remember my credo? Life is short, so enjoy what there is of it. First you have to have that nap. That small strip of beach in the cove is a perfect place—or, if you prefer, I can convert the boat seats into a lying-down position. Won't you rest better if you're not surrounded by undone work?"

"No!"

"You may as well go along with it, Lacey, because it's my small reward for a week of hot trips into town. I'm absolutely bound and determined to head this way, and I happen to be in the driver's seat. For the moment, the only way for you to get to the Eyrie is to swim."

After a few more faint protests Lacey lapsed into silence. A terrible apprehension had seized her. The shorelines were familiar. Landmarks slid past, catapulting her back into time. A narrow channel, a navigation buoy marking shallow waters, a rocky point covered with blueberry bushes, a place where a half-fallen tree almost brushed the boat. . . .

And then they reached their goal, a small quiet inlet with a narrow sliver of golden sand. Tall pines and maples and tangled vegetation pressed in on all sides, protecting privacy. It was the deserted cove where they had once gone for a skinny dip together. That time the swim had been Lacey's idea. Her cast had come off only a few days before. Except for a few compulsive and comparatively chaste body brushes, and the one breathtaking episode while dancing, Gideon had been trying very hard not to touch her. The electricity had been mostly that of young love, a hopeless, helpless yearning without adult fulfillment.

They had come to this cove for a swim because it was so late in the season, very nearly the time of Canadian Thanksgiving. The waters here were shallow, collecting and retaining more warmth through autumn than deeper parts of the lake would do. Feeling half shy, half bold, and entirely desperate because she knew she would soon have to leave for home, Lacey had dared to remove her bathing suit once she was in the water. Not allowing herself time to think, she had thrown it back into the anchored boat—they had been using the big Ditchburn on that occasion—and she had regretted it at once. The boat ladder had been put out on the starboard side, where Gideon was swimming. He had found her a few minutes later, clinging to the port side of the boat, desperately trying to slide in over its high slippery gunwales and retrieve the bathing suit without being seen. Of course, he had caught her in full view. She had sunk back into the water, utterly mortified. "It's all right," Gideon had said. "I do it often myself." And with a careless abandon intended to set her at her ease, he had removed his own bathing suit and tossed it into the boat.

And this was the cove where they had kissed and clung and would have completed everything if it hadn't been for a sudden autumn storm. The wild lash of rain and the sudden forked lightning lancing across the sky had brought Gideon to his senses, but it was little wonder that they had found their way to the bunkhouse only two nights later.

Gideon stopped the boat and dropped anchor. "I'm in favor of a swim first. How about you?"

"I won't be swimming at all," Lacey said, attempting a detached manner. "You didn't warn me to bring a bathing suit."

"Sorry," Gideon said mildly. "I hadn't remembered that you were so modest. Well, in that case, perhaps we'd better eat first. I've never believed that old wives' tale about swimming on a full stomach. Move for a minute; I'll adjust that seat you're sitting on. We can use the bench to spread out our food."

He also adjusted the seat behind the steering wheel so that there were two narrow upholstered benches, each the length of a person, with a small walking space between. That done, he hauled a Coleman cooler out of a small locker at the front of the boat. "What will you have? Ham sandwiches? Cold chicken? Cheese?"

Lacey's appetite was almost nonexistent, but she picked at Gideon's offerings and accepted the stemmed plastic wineglass in which he poured chilled, sparkling rosé. She couldn't concentrate on his light conversation, when all she could think about was the coming moment when he would remove his clothes. She doubted that he had a bathing suit with him. Already he had unbuttoned his shirt, allowing such breezes as there were to fan him. Lacey tried not to notice, but as she was sitting directly across from him, she could not help seeing that his chest was less smooth than it had been years before. Over the ripple of deep pectoral muscles on his torso lay a heavy furring of dark hair, the mature growth of manhood. It arrowed downward in a lighter drift toward the taut, corded surface of his flat stomach, where it vanished in a few last tantalizing curls. The buckle of his belt mesmerized her, and as often as she jerked her eyes away, she found them creeping back.

"Aren't you hot in that jacket?" he asked casually at one point.

"No." But she was, and Gideon's waistband was not the only cause. There was little wind in this protected spot, and only a few cottony clouds drifting overhead. In the open boat the noon sun beat down with no shade to relieve it, such as there would have been on shore. She could feel the trickle of sweat in the roots of her hair and between her shoulder blades.

At last he cleaned the picnic things away, but to Lacey's relief he made no immediate move to go for a swim. "Ten minutes for the digestion," he remarked as he settled back for a short rest. His arms were splayed easily along the side of the boat, a posture that widened the opening of his shirt. Lacey pulled her knees to her chest and hugged them, a subconsciously defensive position.

"Couldn't we go home now?" she asked. "It's very hot in the sun."

"You could swim over to the beach. There's shade there."

"No, thank you," she said in a stilted voice. "I'm not *that* hot. But I would like to leave."

Gideon regarded her coolly. "Impossible," he said.

She was riveted by something in his tone of voice. "What do you mean?"

"Nothing serious—but there's no way we can leave here until at least one of us has had a swim. Earlier, when I leaned over the edge of the boat to cast the anchor, the ignition key fell out of my pocket. I have to dive for it. Oh, don't worry, it'll be down there on the bottom somewhere, but in the meantime you'll simply have to suffer in the sun. Or if you're in a hurry to get back to the Eyrie, you could help me search."

Lacey didn't have to think very hard to produce the suspicion—no, the certainty—that this was a deliberate ruse. For a moment her head spun crazily, for the lost key advertised Gideon's intent. But then she reminded herself that he couldn't have changed altogether in the intervening years. He might have toughened in some ways, but he was still basically the same person. As a young man he had gone out of his way not to take advantage; as a mature one surely he would not force himself on an unwilling woman.

And nothing, nothing in the world, could make her willing.

A moment later he asked, "How long are you planning to stay in Muskoka?"

Lacey had had time to regain her composure. "I'll be here for a while, I imagine. For one thing, I can see it's just a matter of time for Aunt Edwina. And even if she does improve . . . well, I think I'd have to stay around long enough to make some other arrangement for her. A nursing home, perhaps."

"She'd hate that."

"Yes, I think she would. It makes me sad to say so, but it would be better if she just slipped away."

"I take it there's no reason you have to race back to Pittsburgh."

"Not really. Now that I'm up here, I have other business to attend to—mostly the question of what's to be done about the Eyrie. Aunt Edwina will never be able to use it again. Besides, I have the kind of job that allows me to come and go as I please. I won't be fired for taking a few extra weeks."

Gideon looked at her in narrow-eyed surprise. "I thought you lived the life of the idle rich. Your aunt has always implied . . ."

Lacey sighed. "Yes, I know what she implies. You may as well know, Gideon, it's not true. The only Wynward fortune that exists nowadays is in Aunt Edwina's imagination, and that's the way it's been for years. Most of it went in the Depression. The little that was left, my father lost in a series of bad business ventures. I didn't tell you before because I don't like to shatter Aunt Edwina's little fantasies and illusions of grandeur. They've helped her to feel proud and important all these years. But now that I can see she's not going to recover, there seems to be no particular point in hiding the truth. You're bound to find out soon enough, anyway, because I intend to sell the island. I *have* to sell the island. I just can't afford to keep it up anymore. The taxes have tripled in the past eight years, for one thing. For another, I'm still trying to pay off the cost of the new septic tank. I would have sold years ago if it hadn't been for Aunt Edwina."

He was looking at her strangely. "Then perhaps I've been doing you an injustice all this time."

"Yes, I can imagine what you've been thinking. Why doesn't that rich bitch do something about the upkeep of the cottage? But you know, I haven't been able to afford to fix it up. And I didn't know that Aunt Edwina no longer had help." Lacey lowered her head so that her glossy dark hair swung forward in a long, protective curtain. In one way, it was a relief to have told Gideon this much of the truth; in another way she was angry at herself because it would have been better if he'd had no reason to improve his opinion of her.

She lifted her head again, with hints of hostility in the stubborn tilt of her chin. "Of course, now you understand why it's so important for me to marry money. And the island is going to help me do just that. I desperately need some capital. I've run out of eligible bachelors in Pittsburgh, and I have to start looking farther afield. I have only one qualification I really care about, so it shouldn't be too hard to find a suitable man, once I can start moving in the right circles."

"And what's the qualification?"

"Wealth," she said bluntly.

Gideon watched her for a moment, his face impassive. Lacey felt her skin crawl with the certainty of what he must be thinking of her. She didn't care, she told herself. Maybe he'd feel enough distaste that he'd keep his hands to himself.

"Exactly when are you going to put the island up for sale?"

"Thinking of making an offer, Gideon?"

"I wouldn't mind," he drawled casually, as if it were a matter of indifference. "Not that I care much one way or another, but I happen to be a creature of habit. I don't much like the idea of having to change my summer routine. Most people would turn up their noses at that wreck of a cottage, but my standards aren't too high, and frankly I'm used to the old place by now. If I could rustle up some mortgage money I might be able to swing it—provided your price is realistic. Remember, I'm not a rich man. Besides, those docks I put in did increase the value of the property, and so did the renovations to the bunkhouse. And frankly, I wasn't paid a penny for the work. I even bought the lumber myself, and it was a bit of a strain on my budget at the time. Maybe you'd make some allowance for that. And considering the wretched condition of the place . . ."

She looked at him curiously. She recognized the ploys of a customer trying to bring the price down. "You've been wanting the Eyrie all along, haven't you? And that's why you've spent your summers there."

Gideon laughed. "I confess. You've found me out. Frankly, I'd have done a lot more work around the place, but I saw no point in making the old dump look too salable."

"Put the Eyrie out of your mind, Gideon. You wouldn't be able to afford it."

He pulled a wry face. "Probably not." He spent some moments glumly contemplating the shoreline behind Lacey's shoulder, while she spent some moments contemplating him. She felt on more secure footing now that business was the topic of discussion. Gideon finally asked, "How much do you think you can get for it?"

"One of the local real estate agents has been in touch with me off and on for the past few years. I have to be honest—that's the man I had a meeting with a week ago. He told me he could produce an offer for half a million dollars cash, any time."

Gideon's eyes widened with surprise, and then he frowned. "That sounds far too high," he scoffed. "It's not worth half that. And cash? It must be a pie-in-the-sky offer. I doubt you'll ever see it in writing, with a check attached."

"Stop trying to bring down the evaluation, Gideon. I don't much care whether the offer's in writing or not. I haven't told the agent yet, but I might turn it down."

"Why?"

She hardly knew the answer to that herself. She ought to have accepted. But how could she tell Gideon that she had delayed day after day, simply because it wrenched her to think of selling? The Eyrie was creeping back into her heart, but she didn't want Gideon, of all people, to know it.

Her tone was defiant. "I think I might handle the sale myself, subdivide the island, and make a whole lot more money in the end. You should like that idea. Maybe you can buy the bunkhouse parcel, if it pleases you to stay on."

Gideon was staring at her, his face a study in shock. "Subdivide? The hell I'm pleased. How can you do a thing like that?"

"Easily," she retorted, although it had occurred to her only in that moment.

"You're mad!" he thundered, realizing she was serious. The sound of his outrage filled the small quiet bay. He slammed his hand on the edge of the boat, causing it to swing and sway at anchor. "You can't do it! Think of the trouble. Think of the cost. Think of the paperwork, the surveyors, the bylaws, the lawyers, the . . . goddamn it, Lacey, you'll end up losing your shirt! Take your half million and run, if you must! But don't chop up that land! You don't know what the hell you're doing!"

She tossed her hair. "Don't I? Perhaps I should have told you what business I'm in, Gideon. I sell industrial real estate and I'm very, very good at it. With luck, I may even be able to get the whole island zoned for time-sharing condominiums."

That brought him up abruptly. His nostrils flared dangerously and his jaw muscles worked while he glared at her. And then, with a sudden angry movement, he tore off his shoes, jerked to his feet, wrenched off his shirt, and unzipped his trousers. In one second flat he was stepping out of them.

Lacey wanted the lake to swallow her. The whole thing had happened so quickly that she hadn't had the opportunity to wrench her eyes away. She simply stared as if transfixed. The sight of his nakedness hit her with sledgehammer force.

She hadn't even had time to consider his purpose when he turned his back on her and stepped up onto the narrow teak running board along the boat's edge. His broad bronzed shoulders were taut with anger, his polished buttocks hard and smooth as unyielding marble, his muscled calves rigid with rage. Without a word or a backward glance, he sliced into the water and swam furiously toward the mouth of the inlet.

She stared after him, assailed by flutters of helpless feeling. She had intended to have her attention elsewhere when he undressed. True, it had all happened very quickly, but that didn't prevent her from carrying a potent mental image of his maleness.

Gideon was swimming like a man possessed, knifing through the water until she could see his position only by the sharp white froth left by the piston force of his arms and his feet. Soon the closest spit of land interrupted her line of vision, and she could no longer see even that.

She sat numbly, watching the empty horizon. Nothing happened. Time passed. The white froth of a swimmer did not reappear.

Was he that angry? After nearly a decade of summering on the Eyrie, year after year, in hopes of someday acquiring it, he must find the disappointment infuriating. And yet it was unreasonable to expect her to sell the island for a fraction of its worth. With another buyer in the offing, cash in hand, Gideon would be out of the running anyway. He would fare far better with a subdivision. If the island was chopped into pieces, he should at least be able to acquire the parcel of land on which the bunkhouse was situated. He would cool down as soon as he understood the logic of that. Lacey didn't think she would do it, or could do it, because she couldn't afford to wait for the cash—but the whole idea did make sense.

A pair of loons floated calmly into view, then dived for a meal and resurfaced twenty yards farther along. And still nothing happened, and still time passed.

Did he not plan to return? The seeds of an alarming suspicion began to grow. Had he deserted her as a punishment? He was an excellent swimmer; she remembered that from eight years before. Was it possible that he had decided to swim all the way home? It was a good two miles to the Eyrie, but Gideon was undoubtedly capable of it. He had the endurance and the ability, and at the moment he had the motive too. All the same, it was the height of recklessness to swim unattended in a large open lake where there were many huge, high-powered boats moving so swiftly. Any one of them might run a swimmer down before seeing him.

Occasionally, other boats could be seen in the very far distance. And still nothing happened, and still time passed.

Lacey began to panic. Her heart rose into her throat at the thought of Gideon alone somewhere out there in the lake, courting danger out of foolish anger. The more she thought about it, the more certain she was and the more alarmed she became.

She had been alone for at least twenty minutes when she decided she could bear it no longer. She would have to dive for the key and go looking for him. Quickly, she slipped out of her clothes and knifed into the dark water, too agitated by this time to even notice the cooling benison it conferred on her naked, heated flesh.

The water at this point was not too deep, no more than eight or ten feet. The lake was dark with minerals and forest matter, but the bottom in this particular cove was a clean sandy rock shelf, not muddy ooze. She didn't think the key would be too hard to find. After regaining her breath, she found the anchor line and followed it, pulling herself along, hand by hand, while she watched for the telltale glint of metal. Her long hair rose and swirled like a mermaid's, stirred by the slow currents of her own movement.

She rose to the surface, caught her breath, and tried again. Twice she was distracted by discarded metal tabs from aluminum soft drink cans. On the fifth or sixth dive she finally sighted the small key. It was a dark bronze color, not silvery as she had expected, and she realized she must have passed it by several times.

She retrieved it and allowed the natural buoyancy of her body to carry her to the surface. She turned in the water, catching her breath and her bearings, about to aim for the boat.

And that was when she saw Gideon, and he saw her. In her shock, she dropped the key again.

He had just reached the boat, returning from the circuit on which he had spent his energy and his anger. It hadn't been dangerous, as Lacey had visualized. True, he'd punished her by staying out of sight, but he'd only expended his frustrations by swimming furious circles in the adjoining bay, which was a little less private but, as it was out of the mainstream of lake traffic, equally safe.

But Lacey didn't know that, and her first thought was that he had deliberately tricked her. Her second was that she had to escape. And beyond that, she didn't think at all. She couldn't.

Gideon was shaking the water out of his ears and his hair. "Did you find the key?" he inquired.

Lacey couldn't answer. She could hardly breathe. She saw the water gleaming on his naked shoulders. She saw the sun-sparkled moisture on his strong, sensuous mouth. She saw the faint gleam of naked flesh below the surface, distorted by refractions and shimmering like dull, liquid gold. The image of his maleness returned in full force.

And then she saw him start to move toward her. She turned and lanced toward the shore, as if the very devil were in pursuit.

Chapter Five

She emerged from the water gulping air, on hands and knees because she had swum for all her might until the moment she struck sandy bottom, where the water was only a foot deep. She started to rise to her feet, intending to run for the woods, and in that moment a fist of iron closed around her ankle.

"For God's sake, Lacey! What the hell is the matter with you? This isn't a stranger, it's me— *Gideon!* I'm not going to hurt you."

She tried to pull away, twisting and turning within his grasp, but succeeded only in falling, half on sand, half in shallow water. She sobbed and gasped and rolled onto her back, still desperate to escape, and in the next moment felt hard arms encircle her, locking her flailing hands in place. Gideon's ragged breath struck her face. A leg was thrown over both of hers, weighing heavily so that she had no option but to lie there, panting, shuddering, her wet, bare breasts heaving beneath the weight of him. Her facial muscles were rigid and her teeth were almost chattering. It was like all the dreams of this past week. Dreams and nightmares . . .

Gideon was looking down at her, his eyes darkened with disbelief and puzzlement. "What is it you think I'm going to do to you, Lacey?"

She closed her eyes because his lips were far too close and she couldn't bear to see them, to want them so. The consciousness of his nakedness and hers became a thunder in her blood, a pounding in her vitals, a poison in her brain. She hardly heard Gideon's voice; what she heard instead was his body. The thud of his heart crashing against hers, the harsh rasp of his breath, the twisting of his fingers in her slick wet hair to hold her head still, the shifting of his elbow on sand as he pinioned her in place—these were the sounds that assailed her ears.

Gideon kept speaking, but his words reached her as if from a distance. "I can't very well deny I brought you here deliberately. I thought you might remember what it was like when we were here before, and . . . yes, I hoped the old memories might make you respond. I want you—I admit that. But I want you willing, and if you're not, well then . . . oh, damn. Do you think I'd force the issue?"

It was not thought that had caused her unreasoning race to shore, nor was it thought that guided her now. She had been attempting to run from something most potent, most primitive, most personal. It was herself she feared—not force, not circumstance, not even Gideon. She might have been able to run from him, but she couldn't run from herself. And that was the real panic that froze her veins, caused her traitorous body to feel as if it had been stretched to breaking point on a medieval torture rack.

"Open your eyes, Lacey. Look at me! Do you really think me capable of rape?"

She didn't obey or answer, so he simply held her, his nakedness half flung over hers, hoping that stillness and silence would put an end to her unaccountable panic.

Lacey's long shuddering lessened in time, to be replaced by quivering of a different kind. She could not escape knowledge of the male arms enfolding her, of the warmth of male breath striking her temples, of the feel of a wet male chest pressing on her bare breasts, but she could escape a part of reality by keeping her eyes closed and pretending this wasn't Gideon. It was only another of those dreams, and if she could wake from it he wouldn't be there, he wouldn't be naked, he wouldn't be holding her like this.

But it was no dream. The nightmare quality receded as instincts equally as primal as panic began to flow through her, first in trickles of longing and temptation, then in rivers of desire strong enough to leach away the powerful barriers she had erected in her brain. And then a strong tide swamped her—a swirl of confused, forbidden sensations that overpowered reason and right and inhibition. She told her hips to move away from such close contact with his, told her fingers to push against his chest, told her skin to stop trembling beneath his touch. But her hips and her fingers and her skin would not obey.

For some minutes sex was the last thing on Gideon's mind. He didn't understand the reasons for Lacey's terrible fear, but he knew he must calm her before setting her free. If she crashed naked through the undergrowth, she was bound to injure herself—on tangled bushes, on thorns, perhaps by falling into a patch of poison ivy. And if she emerged naked, wet-haired, and wild-eyed in the clearing of some neighboring cottage, there were bound to be uncomfortable questions that would embarrass not only Lacey, but himself. And how in hell could he explain that he hadn't done a damn thing?

After a time he felt her panic recede, and his consciousness of her womanhood and her vulnerability grew in inverse proportion. His grip on her arms eased, became an undemanding hold instead of simple restraint. He shifted the leg that had been flung across her knees, allowing her freedom to escape if she wished. She didn't try.

"What were you so afraid of?" he murmured quietly, his face hovering closely over hers.

"Myself," she whispered in a torn voice. And although her lips remained parted, quivering as if more words trembled on the brink, no more were spoken. Her eyes were still closed, so that the long curve of lashes against her cheek was a dark curtain between them.

Then, for a time, he managed to quell his normal urges by sheer force of will. But the battle against nature was lost when Lacey's entire body suddenly softened and melted against his, signaling not only the end of fear, but the advent of something else. Soon her lips were moist, her face flushed and feverish, her chin tremulous with longing. Then the burgeoning of his manhood was swift, the growth of need doubly strong simply for being unnaturally constrained. He could no longer conceal evidence of his powerful desire, but he lay quietly, waiting for some sign of shifting or stirring, of compliance or rejection, from the woman who lay in his arms.

Lacey felt the sudden, swollen surge of his body. Slowly, as if in pain, she opened her eyes. They were aching with need and molten with longing, as were her thighs.

"Gideon," she whispered in her torment, touching his arm with her fingers, asking him for solutions she herself felt too weak to provide.

Gideon saw, and felt, and knew the signals of a woman racked with strong sexual desire. He knew she had been running not from him, but from her own sexual responses. She wanted him, and she didn't want to want him. She was desperately fighting the old attraction, perhaps because she feared an entanglement that would interfere with her other plans—plans that Gideon held in deep contempt.

But at this point those thoughts were at a subconscious level, in no way rational. He was swept along on a strong tide of his own need. He desired Lacey Wynward, and he hoped to satisfy his desire. A week of watching her, of being beside her every day, of drinking in her subtle perfume and feeling the cool rejection in her manner, had driven him to the point of smoldering obsession. He had found himself thinking of her night and day, remembering the young girl who had been so shy, so vulnerable, and at times so breathlessly bold. As she had given him no encouragement or circumstance in which to act, he had finally decided to manufacture one. But he had always intended to let her make the first move.

With every instinct in his body Gideon knew he could take Lacey now—quickly and surely, if he was willing to do it without compunction. She wouldn't fight him, he was certain. But he wanted more than that, much more. Before he made love to her, he intended to deepen her response to the point where she would need him without question —wholly, drivingly, desperately—just as he, after a week of erotic imaginings and remembrance of the past, needed her. It was not mere acquiescence he sought; for him simple sexual gratification had never been enough. His pride expected, no, demanded, that she be as much of a partner as he in the act of love. When this day was over, he wanted no recriminations, no remorse, no reason for regret.

He stroked her cheek soothingly, a comforting gesture that brushed the silken surface lightly and seemed to make no demands. But it was only a detour to the response he wished to arouse, for the unhurried progress of his fingers led him in time to her ears. Reaching those erogenous zones, he began to finger and fondle their sensitive lobes, his purpose at last revealed.

She opened her mouth to utter a faint protest, only to feel the words driven out of mind by a gentle incursion of his tongue. Her senses reeled. He ran a slow questing tongue-tip along the inner edges of her lips, the most tentative of caresses. She parted them in helpless invitation, and she moaned—the sound soft, yielding, yet tortured, an involuntary but unwilling offering up of soul and self. The moan spoke her mind more clearly than any words would have done.

Unstopped, he continued to toy with her ears and her mouth. He nibbled at her lips, rubbing and biting the lower edge softly until her tongue reached involuntarily to join in the gentle battle. Then he kissed her more deeply, tenderly, expertly, delving by slow persuasive degrees into the moist inner velvet, using all his experience and all his well-leashed ardor to arouse her fullest response. Passion lurked in those wine-sweet depths, reluctantly answering his probing command.

When Gideon felt the growing urgency in her mouth, when she no longer withheld anything in the kiss, he lifted away, deliberately leaving her with a sense of incompletion. When he met that mouth again, he wanted her to be the aggressor.

Drugged with potent aphrodisiacs, Lacey was suffused with a sense of unreality and yearning and sweet rightness, drawn inexorably back in time. Gideon's lingering kiss had enticed her into a warm, delicious, golden bath of sensory pleasure from which she didn't have the willpower to emerge. The headiness of his masculine taste had mingled with the intoxication of sun and sand and tingling, tangled bare limbs, and these things had created a powerful brew indeed. She felt as if her flesh and her bones had been liquefied into a warm, sensuous honey, a flow of pure distilled sensation, and only some harsh awakening could restore her to the solid substance of reality.

When his mouth lifted away, her eyes came slowly open again, and in them was the pain of her great need.

Gideon's damp furred chest was still hovering over one nipple, touching and teasing it lightly, an intimate little scratch of texture that further contributed to her sense of dizzy impotence. A sweet and sinful breathlessness sapped her strength of mind as she saw his eyes lingering hungrily on the pale curve of her other breast, and knew his next goal. Its sensitive sepia point had long since peaked and hardened with desire, so that the tiny droplet of water on its tip trembled and shimmered in the sun. He lifted one hand and with his fingers he began a slow searching, a sensuous stroking that circled the outer breast very gradually. His lean tanned face hovered close, his smoldering eyes intent upon her breast, so that his warm breath fanned and feathered the curve of milk-pale skin. His tenderness destroyed her, and the soft wiles of his seeking fingers seduced her, and the warmth of his close, strong manhood pressing against her naked hip lured her to ask for only a few more moments of this sweet and terrible temptation. Surely it was not so much to steal a few last seconds from eternity?

The slow words he breathed in praise of her breasts were love potions as potent as the passage of his stirring fingers. "Beautiful," he murmured. "They're like milk and honey . . . I still remember the taste. . . ."

With his thumb, he gently brushed away some grains of sand, then drew closer to the quivering nipple, dragging out the moment to a point of delicious agony before he reached the tiny, shimmering droplet that was his goal.

And then he bent and drank it with his tongue-tip.

Lacey groaned, gasped, moaned, and tried to twist away. The shock of erotic sensation had ended the haze of sinful sensual lassitude that had turned her so shamefully compliant.

It was a weak evasion, and it seemed only to redouble Gideon's ardor. Suddenly he was no longer patient, but passionate in his urgency. His parted mouth was all over her now, finding a hundred little droplets, a hundred little pulses, a hundred little places where passion dwelt.

Her agonized protests were faint, scarcely audible, tiny straws of sanity soon swept away in a great flood of feeling that swamped her entire being.

"No," she whispered feebly, and yet her fingers were wound into his hair, twisting and clutching with a fierce urgency, so that he could not have escaped had he tried. "No, Gideon, you mustn't . . . you mustn't . . ."

"I must," he muttered thickly. "I must. Oh, Lacey, you lovely witch. You drive a man to madness . . . I must, I must . . ."

It was Lacey who was driven to madness. No longer merely compliant, she was alive to his touch, arching to his adventuring mouth, digging her fingers into his shoulders, asking more than he gave. She was helpless in the grip of a passionate maelstrom that caused her senses to wheel and whirl. Low sobs of involuntary sensual pleasure sounded in her throat. His sudden, hot demand for response had taken her by storm. She sucked in her breath sharply as his probing tongue delved into the shadowed, hidden cavity of her navel; as it sought the dark sweetnesses and secrets of her flesh. His seeking hands were blazing over her breasts and imprisoning her hips, commanding her full response, now allowing her no escape. She shuddered and writhed and moaned, and where there should have been rejection, instead there was invitation in every twist and turn of her passion-beleaguered body. He drove her wild with the ministrations of his mouth, so that the whole world became a whirlpool in which she was lost . . . swirling, drowning, being pulled ever downward to disaster by the eddies of some strong, irresistible current that was far more powerful than she.

And then Gideon moved upward again, and his knee probed to find a new lodging place, on the sand between her legs. Suddenly wildly conscious that in one thrust it would be too late, she turned her mouth away when he made a move to capture it with his. She was panting again, rigid with a return of panic.

He groaned as he dragged a line of kisses over her averted jaw. "Kiss me," he commanded thickly, too driven now to believe that she could actually hold back response after the intimacies she had allowed him, after the minutes of wanton abandon when she had arched and quivered with uncontrolled passion. Already he had reached a point of no return after the patience he had exerted. While he held himself poised but in check, waiting for her mouth to join with his, his parted lips urgently bathed her temples and her eyes.

"Gideon, no . . . no! Stop!"

There was a real desperation in the plea, and at last it seemed to reach him. He raised himself on his elbows and grew still, although he didn't yet move away. His eyes were glazed and dark with desire, pained, uncomprehending.

"You must stop," she said more quietly. Her

heart pounded tempestuously, but she knew that only reason could control Gideon now. He was in the dominant position and she had to trust in the decency of his instincts. Looking up at his closely hovering face, feeling the muscled weight of him pinning her to the sand, she was afraid to move lest it be already too late. "I don't want this, Gideon. I know it's been my fault, too, but . . ." She waited until moistness returned to her suddenly dry mouth, for she could see the sudden furious fire leap in his eyes. And she knew he had every right to be angry, after the encouragement she had given, after the intimacies she had permitted.

The oath he uttered was not a pleasant one. "Only a first-class bitch would do a thing like this to a man," he said in a dangerously thickened voice. He seized her hair and his fingers tightened into it roughly, hurting her scalp, dragging her face into alignment with his. He glowered down at her, thunderous emotions darkening his eyes, a man in the dangerous grip of white-hot passion and red-hot anger.

Lacey felt the force of him as if it were already battering inside her. There was a real emotional violence in his voice, and she fought against it with the only weapon at hand, her own vulnerability. Her voice was a whispery plea. "Think what you like of me, but please stop. I beg you, Gideon."

"How the hell could you allow me to do those things, and then . . . *oh, God!* What you ask is inhuman!"

Her words were obstacles sin her parched throat. "I . . . trust you, Gideon . . . I . . . know . . . you wouldn't . . ."

"Commit rape?" The word was harsh, and the

harsh humorless laugh that accompanied it doubled its impact. The possibility was real, a sword hanging in the air, suspended by the slender thread of Gideon's self-control.

"Perhaps I'm not as civilized as you give me credit for," he warned savagely.

She could feel the heavy pulse of his need against her thighs, poised for the moment of possession. She could feel the trembling tension in his knees where they pressed hers apart. She could feel the fury in his fingers.

And then she could see the turbulent battle he began to wage with himself. It was there in the ferocious clench of his jaw, the dull color mounting on his cheekbones, the sheen of salt sweat that started to collect on his brow and trickle over his tanned face in long, slow rivulets that slid down to dampen her throat. For a time he stared at her in mute anguish, and then he closed his eyes and gritted his teeth with effort.

Wildly, she thought of the other dissuasions she could use. And yet some deep intuition told her she wouldn't be needing them; that to use them now would be too hurtful, too damaging to his ego. For the moment Gideon's fierce battle was difficult enough, and some things were best said in dispassion, at times when logic ruled. This crucial moment was no time to add another layer of dark, dangerous, primitive emotions.

At last he rolled away, freeing her. She didn't wait to discuss what had happened. She picked herself off her bed of sand and ran, this time in the direction of the water. Within sixty seconds she was back in the boat, dressing her dripping body in the clothes she had discarded in haste not half an hour before. They clung to her wetly, armor against an involvement she didn't want, an involvement that was against everything she had been taught, everything she believed in. And then she sat down in the low hold of the boat, placed her face in her hands, and started to shake uncontrollably.

Gideon remained face-down on the sand for some minutes, fighting internal battles. The sun punished his back and the sand punished his groin. At last, body quiescent but face utterly grim, he rose to his feet. His loins ached with frustrated passion. He was angry at Lacey—if she hadn't raced for the beach in the first place, none of this would have happened. And then if she hadn't responded, he'd never have let things progress so far.

But he was even angrier with himself, because he realized now that he shouldn't have kissed her, shouldn't have tried to arouse her, shouldn't have brought her here in the first place.

Ten minutes later he'd found the key, climbed back in the boat, and dressed in silence. By then Lacey had restored both seats to an upright position. She was sitting facing the bow of the boat, a proper lady to all outward appearances. As far as Gideon could see, the only signs of the ordeal on the beach were the set paleness of her face and the dripping mass of her dark, wet hair. He himself felt as though he'd been through an oversized emotional wringer.

"Are you all right?" he asked stiffly as he slid into his seat.

"Yes." She didn't look at him. "I'm sorry, Gideon."

"So am I," he said in an expressionless tone achieved at some cost. "Very sorry indeed."

He raised the anchor and started the motor. He moved slowly through the treacherous channel that protected the inlet from traffic, but recklessly revved up to top speed the moment he hit open water. He stood at the wheel, letting the wind hit his face full force in an effort to drive some of the demons from his head. He decided he'd had his fill of Lacey Wynward, one way and another. Life was much less complicated with a simple female like Debbie Halloran, whose needs were straightforward, largely undemanding, and always understandable. Debbie wanted a good time, but she didn't expect much else. She was a woman of a liberated generation and she wanted no ties, no commitments beyond the temporary and the obvious. Perhaps he'd made a mistake in telling her that this summer wasn't about to be a repeat of last.

Lacey intrigued him; she always had. But she was too damn complex, and she sent out too many mixed messages. Melting one moment; freezing the next; panicking without reason; sending out silent invitations with her eyes and her actions, and then denying them with her mouth. And in between she gave off that air of cool touch-me-not inviolability that made a man long to test it, for all the wrong reasons. Not to mention all the other Wynward failings, inherited no doubt from her father or her aunt. He didn't understand Lacey at all, and from now on, he swore to himself, he would leave her strictly alone.

And perhaps he would have, too, if Lacey hadn't decided she could no longer hold her tongue.

She waited until they reached the Eyrie. Gideon angled his boat not into the slip, but toward the outer dock. He left the engine running and held on to a boat ring while she stepped out; it was clear that he intended to take himself right back out into the lake. "Gideon," she said, "please, will you tie up and come and have a drink? It's time we did some talking."

His voice was harsher than he intended it to be. "I don't think there's much to say. I made a mistake, that's all. I shouldn't have taken you to the cove. I suppose you're not going to believe me if I tell you I didn't intend to initiate anything without some sort of encouragement from you. The fact is that I did initiate something—or perhaps we both did—for whatever reason. Believe me, I won't do it again."

"I can't take that chance. Please, come and talk."

"I'd better not." He wished he could keep the bitter gall from his voice, but it crept in, a compound of frustration and self-anger, because he was far more upset by the unsatisfactory interlude than he wanted to admit. "I might not have so much control another time," he added sarcastically.

She looked at him with pained eyes, the luminescent amber troubled and darkened even in the light of the sun. "You will," she said quietly, with more confidence than he himself felt, "when I tell you what I have to say. Please, Gideon. I've been feeding you a lot of lies. If I don't tell you some truths, I don't think I can stay on this island another night."

He looked at her with unconcealed antagonism,

angered anew that she would expect him to listen to anything she had to say. He wanted to hear no weak excuses. "Truths?" His tone was corrosive, skeptical.

"Truths," she repeated simply.

"I don't want to hear them," he said grimly, reaching for his gearshift. Before Lacey could say another word, the boat had become a streak of orange lightning, vanishing into the tree-dark horizon of the lake.

Gideon, Gideon, Gideon, she repeated achingly to herself, thinking that she might not see him again. She had not exaggerated; she knew she must now leave. Good-bye, Gideon . . . flesh of my flesh, blood of my blood, heart of my heart. . . .

If he had been willing to listen, she felt she could have stayed. Once she had put the secrets of the past into his hands, she felt she could trust her safety—the safety of both of them—to his keeping. But if he didn't listen, she couldn't trust anything, least of all herself. How could she risk another sunset on this island, where in the night temptation became a dark soul-destroying force, drawing her to her own half-brother?

Chapter Six

acey's despair would have driven her to leave that same afternoon, but it was not to be. With the Ditchburn and the other boats lying useless in the marina shop, she was dependent on others for transportation. She phoned the marina at once. To her distress, Hobie Hubbard's wife informed her that he wouldn't be able to help, as he had driven off with a boat trailer to deliver a large launch ordered by some customer whose cottage was not on the interconnecting waters of the three major Muskoka lakes. By the time his errand was done, it would be night. And the young boy who worked for the marina couldn't possibly come and fetch her, because for the afternoon he was the only person on hand to man the marina's gas pumps. "And I can't help either," Mrs. Hubbard said. "I have a church tea this afternoon, and I'm in charge of the whole thing."

Lacey started to pack while she thought about her predicament. At last, when no other option came to mind, she decided to call the Hallorans and beg a ride. Debbie might not know it, but if she was the one to oblige, she would be doing herself a favor. She ought to be overjoyed, Lacey decided wryly, at the departure of a threat she probably hadn't even recognized.

But the Hallorans' phone was answered by a young child. "Mommy's sleeping," he piped up. "Daddy's golfing at the club, an' Debbie . . . dunno where she is. Just said she'd be gone for the afternoon an' took off."

Lacey said she would call later and hung up.

Her fingers shook as she packed. She had tried to find a dim glimmer of humor in the fact that Debbie Halloran hadn't recognized a threat. How could she have, when Laccy herself hadn't done so? Or rather she had—but she had thought herself capable of handling anything that might happen. And perhaps she could indeed handle Gideon, who had a good deal of self-control. But it was obvious that she couldn't handle herself. She knew she had been sinfully weak during those minutes in Gideon's arms. And during this past week she had often awakened from her dreams and nightmares in a cold sweat and gone to sit in the darkness of the casement seat, looking out at the moon-drenched path. And the casement with its weakened supports had been the least of the dangers.

Briefly, Lacey considered taking a guest room on the mainland while she continued to visit Aunt Edwina and also attended to the final disposal of the Eyrie. She realized she couldn't afford it for more than a few nights: paying the marina bill had sapped most of her liquid resources. She hadn't worried too much, with a place to stay and the sale of the island in the offing. Perhaps she'd have to accept the cash offer at once, simply in order to leave Muskoka as soon as possible. As to Gideon's desire to own the island . . .

Now she recognized that her reluctance to conclude the other deal had had a great deal to do with him. During this past week she had procrastinated; and the procrastination could have had only one cause. In her heart of hearts she must have been wondering if he might want it.

She hated to sell it out from under him, and yet what choice did she have? She would think about it tomorrow when she was more rational. She didn't believe she would be truly rational again, as long as she remained within his reach.

Close to the supper hour she phoned the Hallorans' cottage again. This time there was no immediate answer. She allowed the phone to ring and ring and ring, and at last Debbie's voice came on the line, sounding breathless and excited.

Lacey's throat was a little dry as she voiced her request, for she didn't want to be asked for explanations.

"Look, I'd like to help you," Debbie apologized hurriedly. "But my brother took the rest of the family to supper at the club, and I'm standing here practically starkers, just wrapped in a towel. I . . . er . . . I was about to have a sauna. Any other time, Lacey, I'd be glad to oblige. But right now I'm busy. Why don't you phone the marina? Or if you want, I'll be free in about two hours. By the time it's dark, my brother should be getting home, too, so . . . well, one way or another, if you don't get help, call back, huh?"

There was nothing to do but wait, for Lacey knew no one else to call. During the party the week before, everyone had been on an instant first-name basis. Despite the free flow of casual invitations to drop in, most people hadn't bothered to introduce themselves fully, and if they had, Lacey couldn't remember the surnames in order to look them up in the thin local phone book.

Her packing already accomplished, she went and huddled in the casement window seat in a small miserable ball, turned not in the direction of the path but in the direction of the lake. Gideon's boat was still not back. It might be parked at his own end of the island, of course. There was no boathouse there, only a small uncovered dock, but after what had happened he might very well decide he'd rather leave his boat in the open.

Or it might be tied up at the Hallorans' dock. Lacey felt sick to think about that possibility, and yet . . . oh, God, how could she care?

For two long hours returning images of the afternoon assaulted her. As she remembered her wanton abandon, she felt physically ill. Alternately she shivered with chill and grew damp with the heat of unwanted memories. Tortured visions of hot sun and twined flesh were interspersed with equally distressing thoughts of dark, steamy saunas.

When she phoned the Hallorans again, there was no answer at all. She tried again half an hour later. And again another half hour later.

Sunset came, and then dusk, and the time of greatest danger was upon her. She knew she became less rational in the witching hours of night, when memories of that long-ago romance with Gideon washed through her. Then she would remember how he had thrown pebbles at her window, knowing she was to leave the next afternoon. She would remember how she had slipped out to meet him in her thin cotton nightgown, shivering, ghost-pale under the thin sickle of an October moon. She would remember the sweet rightness of melting into his arms in the resin-scented night, the possessive depth of his kiss when their eager mouths joined in a promise of what was to come. No words had been spoken, for none were needed. She would remember how they had mounted the path, clinging, urgent, already reaching for each other with hasty, hungry fingers, lovers in everything but the final act. She had been so desperately and so headily in love with him, and so blindly happy in that love. Gradually that autumn, she had also grown into a slow surety that Gideon was in love with her, that he was withholding the words only because he felt he was too young to say them. She would have given him the sun and the stars and the universe if she could, and failing that, she had been ready to give herself. She hadn't wanted to wait for his words, and she hadn't thought of the future.

But Aunt Edwina's vigilance had put a sudden, swift, stunning end to all that. For some weeks, it turned out, she had been aware of Lacey's doelike devotion. She hadn't worried unduly because she had also seen that Gideon was holding himself aloof, not encouraging an involvement. Belatedly, only a day or so before, Aunt Edwina had woken to the dangers. Then she had cautioned Lacey against becoming involved, and she had also made travel arrangements for her niece's immediate return to Pittsburgh. But she still hadn't spoken the truth because she hadn't wanted to reveal the family skeletons unless absolutely necessary.

And it had become necessary, Aunt Edwina said, on that last night.

The truth, when Lacey discovered it, had been like a body blow—a bruising, brutal battering ram of truth that had driven home for all time the fact that young dreams of hope and love were not to be trusted. A hellfire of guilt had consumed her. There had been pain and a helpless anger, too, because she knew she had been an innocent victim of the sins and the silences of others. Had she been armed with the knowledge that Gideon was her brother, she felt, she would never have known such longings. The powerful taboos that forbade physical attraction between siblings would have protected her, given her immunity, made her inviolate. Knowing the truth, she could have learned to love Gideon innocently, with emotions that were platonic and clean and pure, not tarred by the brush of carnality.

But by the time she learned the truth, it had been too late for innocence. When Aunt Edwina interrupted, Lacey had no longer been a virgin.

In due course she had grown to believe that the unnatural attraction had been merely the result of youth and inexperience. Nevertheless, from that time on, she had never again been sure of her natural instincts where men were concerned. How many other bastards had been born to her womanizing father? Might she someday be attracted to another? Was this man's tall stature significant, or that man's turn of jaw? Had there been a faint gleam of displeasure in her father's eyes when she introduced so-and-so, who was the son of old Pittsburgh friends? She had held off suitors and broken two engagements because of her own deep doubts.

As far as her feelings for Gideon were concerned, the passage of nearly a decade had lulled her. When she had first seen him a week before, she had at once realized that he still exerted a dangerous hold over her senses. The restless nights since had confirmed it. But until today she had thought herself able to resist his magnetism. Now she knew she was able to resist nothing. When temptation called, her feeble body had answered, and her few faint protests had been belied by her behavior. She was no longer an innocent victim; she was a victim of herself.

Not least of the guilts she bore was that, in those first fatal moments on the shore, before the embraces began, she hadn't told Gideon of the potent social interdiction against his lovemaking. She could have spoken then, before passion changed and charged the atmosphere. But she hadn't; and she didn't dare to dwell on her reasons for keeping silent at that point.

She tried the Hallorans' phone once again, when it was completely dark. Someone answered, but she hung up quickly, heart thudding, and hardly knew why she had done it.

And then she returned to the casement seat, curled into place, and looked out at the faint tracery of black trees against a black star-pricked sky. The path was black, too, because the moon was not yet out. Realizing which view she had inadvertently chosen, she laid her head back and gave in to deepest despair. The living room was also dark, in keeping with her mood. What was fate trying to force her to do?

She sat there for hours, still dressed in the dark clothes she had worn all day. Midnight came and went, the tick of minutes on her watch told by the pale illumination of the newly risen moon. One o'clock came and went. Two o'clock . . . and the moving moon still moved, and the siren shadows of the tall trees still called, and the path through the Eyrie still beckoned to her senses. It tugged at her obsessively, pulling her toward Gideon. Toward some ultimate, nameless act. . . .

At last she slept, exhausted in body and mind, bewilderingly lost in the black and murky hell of her own soul.

She woke sharply, dragged back to instant wakefulness by the sudden switching on of a light and the gruff sound of an angry voice. She hadn't heard what Gideon said, and she turned with the alarmed question written in her eyes.

"I told you never to sit in that window again. What the hell d'you think you're doing? You know how it projects! And the damn timbers that hold it up are rotten right through. It's a miracle that the wretched thing holds your weight at all. Come out of there at once."

She was about to, but then she shrank back. There was a perverse safety in staying where she was. There was a faint whisky aroma in the air, suggesting that Gideon might have been drinking. He looked and sounded stone sober, and he was fully dressed in a black turtleneck and dark trousers, but there was danger in the angry golden smolder of his eyes. They burned with a reckless fire.

"What time is it?"

"Three o'clock in the morning. Damn you, Lacey, move. Out of there this minute!"

She licked her lips to wet them, taking time to answer while she marshaled her thoughts. She didn't obey Gideon's harsh command. "What are you doing here?"

"You said you wanted to speak to me, didn't you?" His voice was sarcastic. "I may not be burning with curiosity to hear what you have to say, but at the moment that's excuse enough for my presence. You invited me and here I am. Out of the window, Lacey."

Her breath felt shallow, constricted. "Why else are you here?"

"If you don't know, then you have less imagination than I would have given you credit for. Now move!"

"No," she said, drawing even farther back. She pulled in a deep breath that pained her lungs. "Have you been with Debbie Halloran?"

Gideon answered bluntly, with measured cruelty. "I would be, right this minute," he said, "but for one small circumstance. Debbie's not the type to sit around and pine. She had a date today, with another man. Do you really think I'd be here if I'd been with her? I may not be a saint, but I'm not a satyr either. One woman a day is enough for me. Out of there, Lacey."

"Do you always come calling in the middle of the night?"

"Be damn glad that I did. Otherwise your rude awakening might have been a very final one indeed. Move!"

"Gideon . . ."

"Get out of the window, Lacey," he warned tightly.

She huddled her legs into the circle of her arms, conscious that his intentions were not entirely honorable. "Exactly why are you here, Gideon?"

"Out!" he barked.

She managed to keep her voice low, level and controlled. "No, I won't come out. I'll sit here while we talk."

"I'm not interested in talk—lies, truths, or anything else. I've been doing a good deal of thinking, and all my thoughts point in one direction. You stopped me this afternoon, Lacey—but I think that's only because you'd had some moments of quivering ecstasy that satisfied *you*. If you'd really wanted to run from me, I gave you all the opportunity in the world at the start. Why didn't you take it? Were you swept away with passion? Well, dammit, so was I! A woman does have *some* responsibility when she allows a man to go so far. But you took what you wanted and gave nothing in return. I don't like being made a fool of, and I don't like being left dangling. Now out of the window, or I'll come in and get you. And believe me, neither of us is very likely to survive that."

"Listen, Gideon—"

He took a few steps forward, his eyes burning into her. "In my present state of mind, Lacey Wynward, I don't particularly care if that casement collapses with me in it."

She leaned forward urgently. "Gideon, listen! I stopped you today because I had to. Because you're my own brother!"

That brought him up short, but only for a moment. He laughed harshly and advanced another step. "You're mad. Do you think I'm going to buy an inane line like that? You're only trying to keep me away."

"Yes, I am—because you're my brother! And for no other reason! Stay where you are, Gideon. I'll come out—if you promise not to touch me." She spoke in a rush and pleaded with her eyes, desperate to reach him before he reached her. "Promise!"

"Like hell! I'll touch you if I want. Only this time I'll give you no satisfaction until you give me mine." He was still advancing, though he was taking a roundabout approach, his lean body panther-like, his eyes fixed on her with burning purpose. He was deliberately stalking her from one side of the window, hoping to scare her out of her niche.

Lacey felt frozen, realizing he hadn't believed her. What could she say to convince him? Once he touched her, she would be lost.

His low, sinuous words were paced to his slow, measured footfall, warnings to move before he entered the precarious projection. "I'll kiss you, arouse you, bring you to a white-hot heat. . . . Like it or not, Lacey," he growled softly, "you're going to respond, just as you responded before. You're a passionate woman and you won't be able to help yourself. I intend to make damn sure you can't."

Lacey used the only instant maneuver she could think of. She sprang to her feet and faced him squarely, knowing he wouldn't expect that. "You couldn't do that to your sister! And I am your *sister*, Gideon! I'm not lying and I can prove it!"

He came to a halt and stared at her. Her extreme intensity had at last stopped him, like a large dam of resistance meeting the great river flow of his anger. That anger had been roiling through his system for the past twelve hours, looking for release. In the small hours of the night, as he remembered the wanton encouragement of her hips, the trembling enticement of her lips, the urgency with which her hands had searched his shoulders and his chest and his thighs, he had become maddened to the point of insanity. She had taken pleasures and then withheld them from him at the very last moment; he felt he had been used in a despicable way. When she had spoken of truths, he had expected she meant excuses. And that had enraged him most of all.

But this couldn't be the truth she had talked of!

"You're mad," he repeated, his voice ragged with disbelief. His eyes were deeply stricken and his face was beginning to turn ashen beneath the tan.

She stared back at him as the terrible revelation hovered, trembled, clung in the air, so that the atmosphere between them became fraught with something new, unnatural, unholy.

"It's true, Gideon," she whispered when the silence had become cloying. "We're half-sister and half-brother, the two of us. Aunt Edwina told me years ago."

"Oh, God," he muttered, in true anguish. He was shaken, the tremble of his hands visible. With difficulty, he remembered other concerns and spoke again with forced control. "Come on out of that window, Lacey, for your own sake. I still think you're mad, but we'll talk. And I won't touch you, I promise. At least, not until"—for just a moment his voice had a cracked quality to it—"until we've disposed of this nonsense."

She slipped out of the window and went to sit in a deep couch, curling herself into it in the same, almost fetal position she had taken up in the window seat. Having shared the awful knowledge she had held so long in her heart, she felt a little safer now, for she was no longer the only one to bear the dual burdens of past guilt and future responsibility.

Gideon remained on his feet, but he walked to the fireplace, where he could lean against the rough stone for support. For a moment he stood quietly, bracing himself against the mantel, his head bent and his shoulders tense. Lacey guessed that he anticipated disbelieving everything she told him; that he was already pre-guessing what she was going to say, preparing himself to shoot down every fact and every circumstance she had in her possession.

Finally he turned to face her. "I think you'd better explain," he said hoarsely. "What exactly did your aunt Edwina tell you?"

She straightened and faced him tensely, with her fingers locked together for strength. She hated to deliver the hurtful news, which would be a second shock to Gideon's system. He had been very fond of his mother; she remembered that from years before. "She's a wonderful woman," he had said once. He had spoken in the present tense, because his mother had been alive then. "She's quiet, loyal, very brave in her own way, for she hasn't had an easy life. She was brought up with scads of money, but she married my father for love—and he was the feckless fourth son of a fourth son, who didn't inherit a penny. Her family consented but didn't exactly approve; they cut off her inheritance. Then my father died when they'd been married only months, leaving her nothing except a newborn child to support. She did it, too, although she'd been brought up to expect a life of luxury and leisure. She rolled up her sleeves and ran a catering service. And she'd never even been taught to boil water." He had laughed. "Actually, she still can't. She just runs the business for the women who can. She may not be everybody's idea of Mom and apple pie, but she's mine. You'd like her, Lacey."

Remembering the warm affection and respect he had had for that central person in his life, Lacey decided that nothing would soften the blow. And he must have guessed by now, anyway, for a sibling relationship could have transpired in no other way. She said levelly, "My father had an affair with your mother."

She could see his chalky face turn even chalkier. She started to speak quickly, unable to offer comfort. "It was a summer thing, up here in Muskoka. You were born in April, weren't you, Gideon? You were conceived in July. Before the summer was over, your mother knew she was pregnant—"

"By my father!"

"By mine," she contradicted, hardly daring to meet his eyes for the outrage and fury she saw there.

"That's not true," he grated heatedly.

Lacey was trembling, feeling her way through an obstacle course from which there was no easy escape. "She married your father because she had to marry someone. In those days it wasn't exactly respectable to produce a child out of wedlock. And my father wouldn't propose to her, because by that summer he was already engaged to be married—to *my* mother." She laced her fingers around her knees to stop them from shaking. "Your mother was in a spot. And so she settled for the next best thing—a man who was willing to admit paternity, perhaps because he hoped to marry wealth. That's what Aunt Edwina said, anyway. Your mother's family put a grudging seal of approval on the marriage only because . . . because they had no choice. They didn't want a scandal. Anyway, although they may have had their suspicions, they had no proof about who the real father was. They were happy to have things hushed up."

"I don't believe a word of this!"

"Did your father ever come to Muskoka, Gideon? According to my aunt, there were no Jerrolds on the Muskoka lakes—only Llewelyns. Your mother summered up here, but your father never did. Think of your birth date, Gideon. Think of when you must have been conceived. Think of the date of your mother's marriage. Think . . ."

Gideon's face was a study. She could see all those thoughts churning, boiling, burning, like corrosive acid etching into his brain. She waited for a while and then added very quietly, "It was hard for me, too, Gideon. I had never known my father was a womanizer. Your mother wasn't the only one he became involved with. There were others, my aunt told me, and I later found out it was true. Oh, he was very discreet about his affairs. He's a little like Aunt Edwina, you know—or he was, until he had his stroke. He used to live one life and talk another. At heart he was a turn-of-the century philanderer, with not so very much respectability at all. He liked women far too much. In fact, I found out later that was one of the reasons my mother had left him."

Gideon's knuckles were white. "I don't give a damn what other women he had! He was not involved with *my mother!*"

He still intended to disbelieve. For her own peace of mind and physical safety, Lacey felt she had to convince him. "Aunt Edwina said your mother used to slip out and meet my father in a gazebo . . . was there a gazebo at the cottage that burned down?"

Gideon glared at Lacey, his jaw working. They both knew full well that there had been a gazebo. He looked as though he wanted to hit her. "It's not true," he hissed. "None of it."

"But it is, Gideon. Remember that remark Aunt Edwina made in the hospital? 'I've forgiven your mother, invited her to the wedding . . .' Something of that sort? Didn't you wonder what that meant at the time?"

"No! I knew what it meant. Your aunt didn't approve because my mother used to work for a living. When I was a little more than a year old—the summer of your father's wedding, I believe—she had actually been working in a restaurant for nearly a year. She washed dishes, Lacey!

Your aunt considered that degrading. She's told me so a thousand times."

"There was more to it than that, Gideon," Lacey said gently and with sorrow, because she hated to see the angry hurt growing in his face. She then told him the things that had convinced her years before—finally, firmly, and irrevocably. "I ran away because Aunt Edwina told me all these bald facts I've just given you. She hadn't wanted me to ask my father about it, but I . . . I did. Later that year. I asked him if you were his son. He denied it, of course. But . . . but he seemed quite upset that I had asked. And he did say I shouldn't get involved with you. In fact, when I told him you'd proposed, he turned quite apoplectic and forbade me to see you again."

"Naturally! You were only seventeen! And would he have wanted you marrying a pauper? A young man with no prospects?"

"Maybe not. But it was enough to convince me." Her eyes dropped. "And later, after he had his stroke, I found a snapshot of your mother in his desk, along with some other mementos of her. There was also a note she wrote him. In it she told him she was pregnant, and she asked him what to do."

"You lie!"

In the back of her eyes Lacey felt the threatening shimmer of tears. She applied the pressure of her fingertips to the bridge of her nose, one forefinger flattened on each side, successfully stemming the flow before it started. "Do you think so, Gideon? Do you? Then why do you think I ran? I didn't care about wealth, position, anything. Those were just excuses." She had been looking at her lap, but now that she had her swimming vision under control her eyes lifted, meeting his. "If nothing else convinces you, think of this. I loved you then. *I loved you.* And I wouldn't have been able to stay away if I hadn't been thoroughly convinced myself. My father was involved with your mother, and you were the result."

"She wasn't like that," Gideon cut in, but his voice was tattered and roughened with the effort of maintaining the fiction that his disbelief was total. His face was no longer ashen. A dull brick color had risen high along the ridge of his cheekbones, a sign that the worst of the shock had passed, to be replaced by other, equally difficult emotions. Lacey herself had gone through that phase of anger and denial.

"I'm sure she was a fine woman," Lacey said, aching for the pain she saw in his eyes. "She may have truly loved my father."

Gideon's eyes were locked with hers for some anguished seconds while time seemed to halt. Then he turned and smashed his fist against the stone fireplace, uttered a foul curse against the heavens, and strode from the room.

He didn't leave the cottage. Lacey heard the splash of water from the bathroom and guessed that he was dousing his face, trying to wash away the stain of what he had learned. She guessed because she had done it herself years before—standing at the sink, laving icy water against her hot cheeks, seeking reasons, seeking excuses, seeking escape from knowledge, seeking relief, finding none. The stain could not be washed away, for it went deeper than skin—it reached down into the veins, the blood, the very vitals.

He was gone for a long time, the continuously running water a testament to the depth and difficulty of his feelings. Lacey didn't follow or try to offer comfort, because she knew she couldn't. Gideon wouldn't thank her for trying; he would be torn with emotions he wouldn't want her to see. Lacey remembered only too well how it had been for her—the face contorted with pain, the dry retching in the stomach, the ghastly waves of sensation that kept sweeping through the entire body with the impact of physical force. She had felt dreadful, sickened, sullied by her part in a love that had seemed so right and pure and natural only a few short hours before. She would not have wanted Gideon to see her in that moment, any more than he would want her to see him now.

He was calmer when he returned. His face was dry, wiped clean of water as well as expression, but his hair was still damp and unruly, evidence that Lacey's guess had not been incorrect. It looked wet all over, as though he had doused his whole head. A thin towel was wrapped around the fist he had smashed against the fireplace.

His facial muscles looked stiff, as though they had been baked and hardened in a mold. He wanted to reveal nothing of himself; she recognized that feeling too.

Watching him, Lacey realized with a sense of dull release that his journey into torment had eased the pain of hers. She could not deny that her feelings for Gideon were anything but sisterly; however, she no longer felt so racked with uncontrollable longings. Some strength had come with the sharing, as she had expected it would. She had wanted to spare Gideon, but now that he knew, she felt selfishly relieved for her own sake.

He dropped into a chair, carefully distant from Lacey, and didn't look at her directly. His voice had become deathly quiet, quite unfriendly. "I can understand why you held your tongue and ran as a young girl. But you're an adult now, Lacey. You knew I was attracted. I can't believe all this is true, or you would have told me a week ago."

"I didn't tell you partly because I thought I could handle it," she said, "and partly . . . partly for reasons of family honor. Years ago I promised Aunt Edwina I wouldn't tell a soul. It doesn't reflect very favorably on my father, after all. I guess I have the fault of the Wynward pride—you know, appearances at all costs. I hate to admit the family sins and failings. The whole thing is very personal and very painful for me, and frankly I didn't want you to know unless it became absolutely necessary. But most of all, I"—she caught her breath—"I didn't want to hurt you. It's hard to tell a man that his mother was unchaste."

"Very touching," he said. His voice was under icy control. "But I still doubt you. If you'd told me at no other time, I'm surprised you didn't blurt it out this afternoon."

"Should I have done that, Gideon?" Her throat hurt, because she knew he was right. And yet she could not have altered her behavior, any more than the planets could alter their course. "Perhaps I should. But I'm also human and flawed. By the time I was over my fright, I had other feelings to cope with. Feelings I shouldn't have had. Once they took control, I . . . couldn't seem to stop, or speak, or think, or—"

He frowned, the first break in his mask. "Never mind explaining," he cut in roughly. At the moment he couldn't deal with Lacey's feelings, only with his own. He turned his eyes to the mantel, where the picture of Lacey's father shared space with all the other Wynward family portraits. "I'm not ready to take your word for all this. Your father denied it, you said. And my mother wasn't the type to tangle with a man engaged to be married. At the moment that's doubt enough for me."

"You'll change your mind once you've thought things through."

"Will I? There's a third question mark in my mind, and it's the biggest one of all. Your aunt Edwina wouldn't have approved of your getting involved with a penniless pup, as she used to call me. She wouldn't have approved of *any* penniless pup, any more than your father would have. She wanted you to marry money, acceptability, position. Doesn't it occur to you that she might have used a falsehood—the first falsehood that came to mind? Or that she might have been *mistaken?* Even if some wretched affair had been going on—which I doubt!—nobody, *nobody,* would have told a maiden aunt about it. Especially your aunt Edwina, who's always lived in another century."

It had indeed occurred to Lacey, years before, once her head had become capable of thought. Aunt Edwina had always made it clear enough that she expected her niece to restore the family fortunes with a suitable match. She could have been trying to engineer a separation. But too many details had seemed to confirm the story.

Gideon tilted his head against the back of his chair. Suddenly he looked utterly drained. "So far I've heard nothing that convinces me," he said tonelessly. "Before I even begin to believe you, I'd want some sort of independent corroboration."

"From where?" Lacey asked dully. "From my father? He hasn't been able to communicate properly since his stroke. From Aunt Edwina? You've seen how she is. And everyone else involved is dead."

"I'll think of something."

"Accept it, Gideon. You'll find it's easier in the long run. And if you could see that note your mother wrote . . ."

He straightened and stared at her with an antagonism that gradually became volcanic. "Accept . . . !" His grip on the arm of the chair tensed and untensed, ferocity in the tendons of his fingers. "I'll do nothing of the sort. I accept nothing and neither should you. Your aunt Edwina was mistaken—*or lying*. Dammit, Lacey, how can you be so gullible?"

His furious denial had restored some of her anguish; it would be hard for her if he didn't come to terms with the truth. Although Lacey understood Gideon's explosive feelings, it seemed the final straw that he should be expressing such intense anger at her, about a situation she didn't want, hadn't created, and couldn't change.

"Gideon," she whispered, "our eyes. Think of our eyes. The same color . . . it's my father's color too."

That had been Aunt Edwina's final telling point, a potent one indeed for Lacey all those many years ago. How could she forget her own shy comment on the similarity between Gideon's eye color and her own? She had noticed it the first time they had exchanged tentative glances.

"God," he lashed out, "how many people in the world have brown eyes? I inherited those from my mother. If you're so damn convinced, Lacey Wynward, *why in hell did you let me make love to you?"*

He glared at Lacey, gold glinting in the angry brown depths of his eyes, jaw working furiously, until he saw that the glint in her eyes was not the glint of amber but the wet shimmer of tears. She was fighting them, and losing.

For a moment those tears angered him, for they seemed to signify a release he himself couldn't indulge in. "My God, Lacey, don't pretend innocence! You weren't exactly pure during that entire encounter. By the name of all that's holy—"

"What's holy?" she cried. "Nothing's holy, Gideon! *I'm* not holy! And how can you expect me to be pure? That innocence you speak of—if you remember, I lost it eight years ago!"

The tears could no longer be held back or concealed. It was a weakness perhaps, but the past days and nights had been difficult ones indeed. With dark hair streaming down over her shoulders, she bent her head into her hands and gave in to the desperate flow.

Gideon was across the room in seconds. He came down beside her on the couch, pulled her head against his chest, and cradled it with one hand. His other hand stroked her shoulders softly, a gentle and undemanding caress. It broke the spirit of no promises, for there was no eroticism in the touch, only warmth and understanding.

She was crying for him and for herself, but most of all she was crying for the terrible physical weakness she had shown during the time in the concealed cove. Knowledge had given her a guilt that Gideon didn't have to share. What had happened between them was her shame alone.

"It's not true, Lacey," he muttered huskily after a long, long time, when her tears had slowed and exhaustion had turned her body to a leaden weight against him. She was still clinging, still unwilling to let him go, not out of sexual torment this time, but because she needed a comfort and forgiveness only he could give.

How could she ask for comfort from Gideon, who must need comfort himself? And yet she had done so, and he had given it. The warmth that gradually stole through her heart bore no relation to the warmth she had felt during the sinful afternoon.

She had no fears that the embrace would lead to intimacies. With puffy reddened eyes and stinging cheeks, she would appeal to no man. Moreover, all desire had been burned out of her by the past hour's happenings. She thought it had been burned out of Gideon too. His quiet hold had been the hold of a brother, no more.

"It's not true . . . not true . . . not true . . ."

In a whisper, he kept repeating it against her ear. She did not know if he was denying her fall from innocence, or that of his mother. It seemed unimportant. The slow murmur, like quiet waves lapping against a sheltered shore, lulled her into restfulness.

Before they slept, wrapped in each other's arms, some measure of inner peace came to Lacey. She had realized that a great, great part of her love for Gideon was pure.

Chapter Seven

$\mathcal{W}$akefulness came to Lacey near noon the next day, brought on by sounds of approaching horsepower, waves slapping softly against the dock, and a motor being cut. A boat had landed at the Eyrie.

Gideon was no longer stretched alongside her, and from the coffee aroma in the air, she thought she knew where he must have gone. She uncurled from the couch and pushed her tangled hair out of eyes that felt puffy and gritty, almost as if they contained tiny granules of sand. It was excessive dryness, the aftermath of long weeping, and she imagined they looked dreadful. Her clothes were twisted and wrinkled, making it obvious that she had slept in them.

She didn't want to see anyone, least of all a casual visitor.

She went to the window—a safe one this time, not the casement—and looked out in time to recognize Hobie Hubbard emerging from the marina launch, his wrinkled walnut face beaming in friendly fashion, but not at her. He was looking along the dock, toward one of the doors on the lower level.

"Hello, Hobie," said a quiet voice. Gideon's. He was out of view. "I was just having a look at this broken door hinge. Er . . . if I'm not mistaken, I believe Miss Wynward may be resting. Earlier this morning she said she had a headache. Can I help you?"

He must have heard the boat's approach, Lacey realized, and gone down to meet it in hopes of preventing too much noise.

Hobie took the hint and kept his voice low. His attitude to all things Wynward had improved considerably since the paying of the long-outstanding bill. "Oh? Mebbe I best speak to her, anyway. I come to pick her up. If she still wants it, that is."

"Pick her up?" Gideon sounded instantly alert, curious. "She wanted a ride somewhere?"

"Jest into town. The wife said as how she sounded pretty urgent yesterday, said she had to git off the island fer some reason. Then we couldn't git through on the phone line this morning, so I thought I'd best come over an' see."

"Perhaps she took the phone off the hook," Gideon said blandly. Lacey decided he must have done it himself; it was unusual for the party line to create no disturbance throughout an entire morning. "Miss Wynward may have needed a boat yesterday, but she doesn't today. If she has to go into town, I'll take her. I have business there myself. Sorry, Hobie, that you had to come out on a wasted trip. How's the old Ditchburn coming along?"

"Cussed thing. Innards need rebuilding, but Miz Wynward younger—Miz Lacey, that is—says she ain't about to have it done." He shook his head dolefully. "Mebbe if you had a word with her, Mr. Jerrold? Shame to let a grand ole thing like that jest molder away. Fix 'er up, she'd sell fer a thousand bucks a foot. Yup. That's the going price these days."

"And to fix her up, it would *cost* a thousand bucks a foot," Gideon said dryly. Fleetingly, Lacey wondered how he could retain any sense of humor at all after what he had learned last night.

Hobie chuckled and clambered back into his launch. "Money ain't what keeps these ole wash-tubs afloat," he said, patting the mahogany dashboard of an old well-preserved Minett, another relic from early in the century. "It's love, jest love. Most folks, they ain't about to reckon the cost, 'cause they'd jest as soon give up the family island. Young feller like you, don't 'spose you'd understand. Seen you runnin' about the lake in one of them spanky new boats. You modern fellers, all hustle and bustle, not like the ole Muskoka folks."

"Actually, I am old Muskoka folks, Hobie. My mother was a Llewelyn."

"Well, was she now!" Hobie brightened and his face creased into a grin. "All these years I known you, an' you never tole me a thing like that? An' I thought you was jest one of them ornery summer people."

"Perhaps you knew her? Peggy Llewelyn? Brown hair, brown eyes, very petite, and quite pretty. When she was young, she had a wonderful smile. A dimple in one cheek."

Lacey knew why Gideon had broached the subject after years of keeping silent. She listened with bated breath, for it seemed to indicate that he accepted nothing. Did he intend to start probing the past?

Hobie seemed to roll the description around in his mind. "Cain't say as I remember," he decided at last. "Be unnatural if I did, I reckon. Them Llewelyns, they used to take their big Seabird to another marina, close over to their own island. Well, well. To think you're one o' the folks, after all. First Llewelyn, that was Jack, he come up here back in . . . well, reckon it must be near a century ago. Bought his island from my own granddaddy."

"Do you mind if I come over and talk to you about it some day? I've decided it's time I started putting together a family history, while there are still a few old-timers who remember."

"Glad to." Hobie grinned. "Any time, any time. Well, see you, young feller. An' I sure am sorry I said no when you asked to open a charge account some years back. Come an' see me any time."

By the time Gideon had trudged back up to the main level of the cottage, Lacey had splashed water on her eyes. She looked awful, and she still felt dull and heavy with the emotional binge of the previous day and night. But at least, she decided, the long horror had ended with some measure of peace. The hours of feeling Gideon close to her, a spiritual closeness with no undertones of the physical, had produced a beneficial effect. She felt she was more in control now, no longer so powerfully pulled in one direction by her mind and in another by her body. In that tug-of-war, she hoped, her mind had at last won.

Not bothering to change, for she didn't much care what she looked like, she walked through to the kitchen. Gideon was sitting at the oilcloth-covered table, nursing a cup of coffee. "You're awake," he said, looking up. "I thought I heard you. How are you feeling this morning?"

"Better."

They looked at each other without smiles, for knowledge still lay heavily between them. And then Lacey looked away, feeling shy in a way she hadn't felt for years. Gideon's expression had been carefully unsuggestive, just as it used to be years before, but for some reason it disturbed her deeply. She wasn't sure why.

"You were going to run away yesterday afternoon," he said.

"I felt I had to."

"And now?"

"I'm thinking about it."

"You're not planning to go today," he said, and it was a statement, not a question.

"I don't know."

"You shouldn't do anything today, and that includes visiting your aunt Edwina."

Lacey thought of her puffy eyes and dark circles and decided that after a straight week of hospital visiting, she could forego the ritual for one day. Aunt Edwina never recognized her anyway. She nodded, but added, "I might move into town, get a room on the mainland for a few days."

"There's no reason you have to leave, Lacey," he said quietly, and she knew he was making a promise of sorts.

She sat down at the table and accepted the cup of coffee Gideon had poured for her. She stared into it. "I couldn't leave Muskoka today even if I wanted to," she said. "First I have a lot of decisions to make—what to do about the island, for one thing. I know I should decide that right away."

Gideon frowned faintly. "I wish you would," he said. "It might help me reach a few decisions too."

She sighed. "I'll try, then. Perhaps the coffee will help clear my mind."

She sipped at it thoughtfully. While she did, Gideon rose to his feet and laid out cheese and fruit and a few other simple things he found in the fridge, a sop to the practical necessity of keeping body and soul together. Lacey, who had not eaten for nearly twenty-four hours, picked at them as she considered her course of action. Gideon kept his silence, leaving her freedom to make her decisions without interference.

She knew she must formulate her plans at once. For the first time in days, despite the heaviness in her head, she seemed to be thinking intelligently. Some emotional logjam had been cleared, freeing the channels of her mind.

The idea of subdivision made good business sense, she knew. She had had all sorts of reasons for tossing it in Gideon's direction yesterday—but it had never been a serious possibility. She couldn't afford to hang on to the Eyrie long enough to go through the paperwork, the council meetings, the legal footwork that would be required in order to break the acreage into parcels.

She had hoped to make a good deal of money on the island, in order to establish a permanent trust fund that would pay for the care of her father. With the requirement for full-time trained help and a good deal of medical attention, that was a fairly expensive proposition. In the event that anything happened to her, she wanted to know he would be well taken care of. But couldn't she buy an insurance policy that would serve the same purpose?

After seeing the Eyrie, after reliving all the old memories and being flooded with the nostalgia of other summers, she realized she would prefer to have it fall into the hands of someone who would restore the old cottage rather than tear it down. Gideon might want to . . . but if he managed to dig up a decent down payment, he could never afford the enormous cost of renovation. So what was the solution to that?

Aunt Edwina . . . that was another problem. Her state of health might remain stable for months, or for mcre days. She would never recover—the doctors had made that quite clear. Lacey decided she couldn't remain tied to Muskoka for an indefinite time, waiting for a final breath that mightn't come for weeks. She could always return when necessity dictated.

So it came down to one decision: what to do with the Eyrie. That was the only thing that really held her in Muskoka.

At last she looked up at Gideon and found his watching eyes upon her, carefully enigmatic, showing no trace of his thoughts. "I've decided to accept your offer on the island," she said.

"*My* offer?" Her unexpected statement stunned Gideon out of his reverie. His brows shot up in surprise, and some coffee splashed onto a saucer as he lowered his cup incautiously, without looking down. He was staring at Lacey incredulously. Of all the options available to her, it was the one he would never, never in the world, have expected her to pick. "How can you be so sure? I haven't even named a price."

"Then name one," she said calmly.

"You're mad!"

"What's mad about it? As you pointed out yourself, it's not in great condition. And you've done some of the repairs yourself, out of your own pocket. And not everyone's in the market for an island. And—"

He was still dumbfounded. "Why on earth would you accept *my* offer?"

"Simply because I want to get back to Pittsburgh as soon as possible."

Gradually he managed to work his startled expression back under control. "No other reason?"

"None at all, except that I'm looking for a very, very quick sale. You name your terms and I imagine I'll agree. I'm sure you'll be fair. If we go to a lawyer this afternoon, I'm certain we can work out the whole—"

"Why are you in such a hurry to leave?" he broke in.

She lifted her hand in a small, fluttering gesture. "I told you, I want to get back to Pittsburgh at once."

"Still running, Lacey?" he asked softly, his eyes fixed on hers. "You can't run all your life, and you can't run away from yourself. If you leave now, you'll always wonder if you lacked the strength of will to stay. I saw how you felt about yourself last night . . . the tears, the self-recrimination, the self-doubt, the torment you've gone through. Wouldn't it be better to stay? You might find out that you're stronger than you know. Are you going to wonder about yourself all your life?"

"It's not . . . only that," she denied weakly. She felt suffocated. "My father . . ."

"He's reached a time of life where he doesn't need a daughter to baby-sit him. Didn't you say he's well cared for?"

"Yes, but—"

"You can fly back at some point and see him, if you must. But you ought to stay here until you get your business sorted out. And your aunt Edwina . . . how can you walk out on her at this point? The nurse says she asks for you occasionally when she's lucid."

"Which is usually in the middle of the night! She might never be lucid by day. Gideon, I *can't* stay." Her anguish could not be concealed. "Don't you understand?"

His mouth was grave, his eyes intent. "You're perfectly safe on this island, Lacey. Don't you trust me? After yesterday and last night, you should."

With an effort, Lacey reminded herself that this was a cottage sale under discussion; she didn't have to allow Gideon to guide the conversation. She steadied herself by taking a hard grip on the edge of the table. Gradually she forced her face to fall into the mold of competent businesswoman, and when she was ready, she met his gaze levelly. "I have to sell the Eyrie anyway," she said. "Can we talk business?"

"What about that idea of subdivision?"

She made a dismissive gesture. "You were right. I can't afford the legal fees or the long wait. As it happens, I'm flat broke. I've been paying off some of Aunt Edwina's horrendous bills, and it's left me in desperate need of a cash infusion." That was perfectly true.

Gideon's eyes narrowed. "But you have another offer, you said. Half a million cash, any time you want it. What happened to that?"

Still protected by the façade of cool competence, she shrugged. "As you yourself pointed out, it's not in writing. And it might be weeks before it is. Anyway, that real estate agent may have just been fishing, because he suspected the Eyrie would soon come up for sale. Agents will do that, you know. They invent interested customers who fail to materialize for one reason or another, as soon as they get the listing signed, sealed, and delivered. Then all the big hype ends, and they begin to suggest that the deal fell through because the property is overpriced. That's when they start talking you down to a realistic figure. After all, Gideon, I'm in the business, I understand all these tricks."

He was looking at her so strangely that she picked up an orange and began to peel it nervously, giving herself something else to focus on. "Anyhow, this way I can save the agent's fee," she muttered, "so I can afford to sell the island for a good deal less. I'm not giving you anything on a platter, Gideon. I've decided it's the right deal for me. You know, a bird in the hand."

Gideon watched her bent head for another moment, his eyes now shrewd, for he was beginning to understand many things. Then he said bluntly, "You're lying."

Her fingernail bit too deeply into the flesh of the orange, squirting her chin. She wiped away the juice and looked up at him defiantly. "I don't know why you'd think that."

"Because," he said in a grim voice, "you *do* have that offer in writing. With a check attached too. All you have to do is accept the offer, sign on the dotted line, and walk to the bank."

Now it was she who was shaken. She stared at him, unable to comprehend.

"Dammit, Lacey, don't you understand? I made that other offer myself."

"But you . . . but yesterday . . ."

"I was only trying to find out if you were planning to accept the damn thing! I was getting fed up with sitting around waiting for your decision. Hell, I expected you to jump at the chance a week ago—when you first saw the check."

"But your name wasn't on the offer," she whispered, dazed. "And you . . . you wouldn't be able to . . ."

"I decided to act through an intermediary. Is that so unusual? It does happen, you know, and I had my reasons. Are you thinking I couldn't possibly have put up the money? Well, I admit it strained the resources a bit; it's a lot for a man to come up with in one chunk. But I'm not quite as broke as you think."

She looked at him as if he were a stranger from another planet, and at the moment she felt that way. "I guess not," she said feelingly.

In that moment of dazed wonderment, a thousand questions chased through her mind. Had Gideon done better at writing than he'd pretended? Had he inherited money, made a killing in the stock market, won a lottery? And why had he been concealing his true financial state?

She might have asked some of those questions, but he glanced at his watch. "Will you excuse me a moment? I have an urgent phone call I must make."

When he returned a moment later, Gideon calmly supplied some of the answers Lacey had been seeking during his short absence. He sat back down at the table looking well satisfied with himself. With elbows propped on the table, and jaw propped on his hands, he regarded her from beneath hooded eyes, a faint smile hovering over his lips.

"I guess it's time for honesty, isn't it? Now that you've revealed some of your truths—and fictions—perhaps it's time for me to reveal some of mine. My fiction is the kind you read, and it's mostly of a historical bent. It happens that I do very well at it, Lacey, and have for years. Don't bother to go looking on the shelves for my name, because you won't find it. I'm listed as G.J. Llewelyn."

She had seen the name on best-seller lists—yet another small shock for Lacey. G.J. Llewelyn was a serious writer, seriously received, whose work dealt with various eras of history in a sweeping, larger-than-life way. And that was Gideon? He'd done that well?

She had not read any of his books, and said so. "But I'm impressed," she added.

"If you'd actually read them, I might take that as a compliment," Gideon noted with wry irony.

She broke the small awkward silence that followed. "Why do you write under a pseudonym? It's not as if you write something to be ashamed of. You should be proud."

"Elementary, if you think about it. I sold my first book years ago—not long after you ran away, allowing me to think your reasons were purely mercenary. At the time I was very bitter toward you. Frankly, I felt that if I had any success, I didn't want you to learn about it. When I saw the size of the advance that was offered on that first book, I was flabbergasted. I had the idea that if you learned about it, you might turn up on my doorstep someday, having decided I was a little more eligible than you'd believed. I thought I mightn't have the guts to tell you where to get off—and that scared the hell out of me. So . . . I've been using the pen name ever since. I've found it a useful piece of fiction, anyway. It helps me to live a private life. G.J. Llewelyn does have the odd fan, you know." He laughed ruefully. "In fact, some of them are very odd indeed. Your aunt Edwina, bless her head, was one of them. At one point she bought one of the books, hardcover edition, because she didn't like going on a waiting list at a public library. That was too plebeian for her. She got very cross with me because I dared to tell her she shouldn't have wasted her money. She told me she wasn't as much of a wastrel as me, and that if I could write anything one tenth as decent, I might actually manage to make something of myself. After that backhanded compliment, I made sure she got autographed first editions hot from the printing presses."

Lacey surprised herself by laughing, something she could have sworn herself incapable of only a few short hours before. "And how on earth did you explain that to Aunt Edwina?"

"I told her that old G.J. was a distant relation of my mother, happy to learn that he had such a discerning and loyal fan."

Lacey was looking at Gideon curiously, thinking

how little she knew about him, and yet how much. He was making light of his own success, she knew, not of her aunt's foibles. She also wondered inadvertently whether all these revelations of Gideon's were in part an effort to create a new kind of relationship between them, the companionable relationship of brother to sister. The thought made her feel vaguely uneasy, for she knew it couldn't be managed. But his casual manner was intended to set her at her ease, she was sure, and indeed it did help.

"Crazy, isn't it?" he went on. "And all the time your aunt didn't have a clue it was me, until the very end. She happened to pick up the phone while I was talking to my publisher one day. If I didn't know better, I'd almost swear that was what gave her the heart attack." His bantering mood suddenly ceased. "Well, actually, perhaps it did. Not so very long after that, I found her on her bed, prostrate with pain."

After a short sober silence he added, "Would you believe, all this past week I've been afraid she'd let the truth slip in your hearing. I think she—" He stopped as if on the verge of saying more, then frowned to himself. Almost at once he grinned as if to restore the easy atmosphere between them, but something was missing. "A day ago I could have sworn I'd never tell you these things."

Lacey studied the uneaten orange, turning it in her hands. "Why *are* you telling me? Because you know the mercenary little bitch can't possibly . . . turn up on your doorstep, looking for a rich husband?"

Every iota of lightness vanished from Gideon's

manner before he answered. "Because I was wrong about the reason you ran." His voice was a little gruff. "And because I've been wrong about a lot of other things. And because . . . oh, hell, Lacey, isn't it time you dropped the pretense of being mercenary? It's outworn its usefulness, and so have some of your other fictions. Now let's get back to the real question—my offer for your property. I'm retracting it. In fact, that was the phone call I made. I told the agent to rip up the offer, Lacey. I've decided I don't want to buy."

She looked up in surprise and sharp dismay as the bottom dropped out of every one of her plans. "Why not?"

Gideon's expression was cool. "That," he said, looking at her directly, "is none of your business. Will you excuse me, Lacey? I have some important things to attend to."

Chapter Eight

Lacey paced the cottage after he had left, feeling badly shaken and trapped. For the moment she was all businesswoman, and her personal feelings for Gideon had no bearing on her mood. She was angry at him, first for tricking her into thinking that he was making a genuine offer on his own behalf, and then for letting her down. She'd talked about a bird in the hand, but in truth, she had thought she'd had two. Gideon and someone else. She had been sure the cottage was as good as sold, either way.

And then Gideon, damn him, had killed both birds with one stone.

How could he do this to her? It was because she'd admitted that she was flat broke, she supposed. No doubt he thought he could work her down to a *really* low price if he kept her dangling for a while. She should never have told him she was desperate to sell—it was bad business practice.

Damn him anyway! But perhaps he'd be sorry. She would list the cottage with a local real estate agent and find some other buyer altogether.

But if she did that . . . oh, God, how long would it take to sell? She had used practically every last penny of her savings to pay Aunt Edwina's marina bill, with expectations of recouping the money very soon. With no immediate buyer in the offing, she couldn't count on a sale before the summer was through.

It didn't take long to reach the first of her decisions. She had liked the real estate agent she had met, and she still had his business card.

She went to the phone at Aunt Edwina's bedside and found it off the hook. Almost as soon as she hung it up, it started to ring. As it was someone else's signal, she then had to wait until the line was free. At last she reached the agent, told him he had the listing, and suggested an appointment in his office.

"No point in that," he said. "I'll have to come to the island and look it over myself. When would that be convenient?"

"Oh . . . you haven't seen it?" She was disappointed, but not really surprised.

"I'm afraid not. I had the surveyor's report at hand when I wrote up the offer, so it wasn't necessary before. After all, we had a firm . . . what seemed like a firm buyer." The little pause tactfully told Lacey he was disappointed that she hadn't struck while the iron was hot. "This time it won't be so straightforward. I'll need more information, measurements and so forth. And I'll be taking some pictures. A lot of clients won't be bothered making the trip to see the place, if they can't see what the layout's like. That's one of the troubles with islands. When can I see you?"

"This afternoon?"

"I'm afraid not. I don't have a boat myself, and I'll have to arrange for one. Another of the troubles with islands! Tomorrow afternoon?"

They settled on a time. One thing decided. Lacey sank back against the pillow of her aunt Edwina's bed and entered into the next phase of thinking. Should she move into town, take a room for a night or two, as she had considered doing? Perhaps it wouldn't be necessary.

Gideon was right about one thing. If she ran off today, she would be running from self-knowledge. She trusted him; it was only herself she didn't trust. Should she risk it or not?

It took a little longer to reach that decision, and when she did she picked up the phone and called the marina. Hobie Hubbard himself answered. "Why, sure, Miz Wynward," he agreed good-naturedly. "Be glad to pick you up. An' if you don't mind, when I do, I'd like to git some o' the bill settled. Jest so's it don't mount up on you."

"Bill?" asked Lacey, with the sinking feeling that she wasn't going to like this. "You mean . . . for coming out to the island this morning?"

"Clean fergot about that," Hobie said laconically, much to her horror. "Nice o' you to remind me. I'll tote it onto the rest."

"The rest?"

"Why, yes. It's them boats in the shop—Ditchburn, mostly. Bushings shot in the water pump, had to rebuild it. Cain't run her dry, or the engine would've gone for sure. Lucky she ain't done that already! Battery's durn near dead too. An' that ain't all, Miz Wynward. I been near two days in the shop, jest tooling the dinky little parts I ain't able to buy." He droned on with a recitation of the boat's mechanical handicaps, most of them seemingly insoluble without a huge infusion of cash. And he had not even begun on the unstartable Dippy, not to mention the leaky canoe, which was there in hopes that a little caulking would help. Lacey began to realize that she was a mere babe in the woods when it came to the costs of antique boat repair. She hadn't expected anything like this, or she wouldn't have sent the boats in at all.

Before he had a chance to go through the whole list, Lacey interrupted. "Look, Mr. Hubbard, I just remembered something. I'm expecting a phone call this afternoon and I can't go out. So I won't need you after all. I'll come and see you about that bill next time I'm around that way, all right? And in the meantime, don't give the boats any more attention."

She hung up and stared at the phone as if it had been a snake. And then she lay back and fixed her eyes on the ceiling while she thought about spending another night on the island.

She had believed that morning that the worst must be over, but when her skin started to grow clammy she wondered if the hellfire of feelings would return with the fall of dusk.

Her mind had not long turned to the Hallorans when the phone rang again. This time she recognized the signal. She waited until three full rings had finished, conscious that it was really Gideon's line. Finally she picked up when it seemed he wasn't going to answer.

It was Debbie Halloran. After an exchange of pleasantries, Debbie stated her true business. "I'm phoning Gideon, actually. Is he around at that end of the island? He's not in his bunkhouse."

Lacey answered in the negative. "I really don't know where he is, Debbie. His boat's not down in the boathouse, that's all I can tell you. I thought it was tied up at the dock near you."

"It was last night, but it's not now. Oh, damn."

"Shall I give him a message if I see him?"

"Yes! Tell him I'm so *damn* angry I could chew nails and spit rust. First he gets me to break another date for this afternoon, and then what does he do? He stands me up, the arrogant bastard. Well, from now on, if he wants a sauna, he'd better go to a health club. Or even better, forget the steam and just go jump in the lake. Preferably in the middle of winter. And you can tell him I said so."

"Maybe he got delayed somewhere."

"Maybe, but . . . could you hold a minute, Lacey?" She came back on the line in seconds, sounding a lot happier. "Don't bother telling him anything," she said with laughter in her voice. "I'm about to tell him myself."

So those were Gideon's plans for the afternoon. Lacey wasn't particularly happy to know, but at least they made her feel a little easier about her own. As it seemed that fate was practically forcing her to stay overnight on the island with him, it was a good thing that at least one of them would not be in a state of deprivation.

She put on a bathing suit and dragged herself

down to the lake for a swim and a healing soak in the sun.

Later in the day, still lying alone on the dock, she saw the soaring rainbow kite of Debbie's ski boat, and after some moments of squinting decided the lean bronzed figure in the sky was Gideon's.

Why should she begrudge him that? Or the sauna? Or the company of another woman, which after yesterday he must sorely need? She should have been glad that Gideon wasn't pining for something he couldn't have.

It gave her little comfort. And yet she was calm when she went to bed that night—despondent, dispirited, depressed, but calm. For the first time in days she slept soundly.

Morning brought a visit to Aunt Edwina, the marine part of the trip courtesy of Gideon. For the first time he also offered his car. Lacey realized why he'd never suggested it before. It was a sleek dark blue BMW she'd seen in the parking lot, hardly the car of a pauper. She refused the offer and headed for her own Ford sedan.

On the way to the hospital they seemed to have very little to say to each other. He didn't ask her plans, and she didn't ask his.

Aunt Edwina was about the same—rambling, dreaming of the past, mumbling about a future grandeur she would most surely never see. With a sense of dull realization that couldn't quite be called surprise, Lacey recognized something she had never recognized before, something that, added to other reasons, helped explain why she hadn't returned to the Eyrie for so long. She'd been angry at Aunt Edwina for years. The suppressed anger had not been because of a lonely old woman's pretenses, her pretensions, or her pride. Those were sad, small sins. They deserved pity, not anger.

The anger was simply because Aunt Edwina had hidden the truth for too long. The sad, small sins that had caused her to hold her tongue, protecting family secrets, had given birth to a large dark sin, a sin against nature. Had her aunt not been so secretive, Lacey knew that she herself might have been spared the larger part of a long emotional ordeal. But Aunt Edwina had become alarmed too late, had arrived too late, spoken too late . . . and the act she had failed to prevent had blighted Lacey's entire adult life.

Maybe now that she had recognized the anger, she could start putting it behind her. It would be nice to forgive an old woman before she died.

But when she turned away from the hospital bed and met Gideon's eyes, those eyes that were so like hers, she knew it was going to be hard. Aunt Edwina had a lot to answer for.

On the return trip in the boat Lacey mentioned the appointment with the real estate agent, hoping to prod Gideon into a restoration of his offer on the cottage. He nodded gravely but made only one comment. "I won't be able to show him through the bunkhouse, so you'll have to do it yourself," he said levelly. "I'm busy this afternoon."

"More steam heat?" she asked, immediately regretting the small bite in her voice.

"Maybe." His tone was noncommittal.

Lacey decided he must have another date with Debbie. That was good news, she scolded herself, and she ought to be encouraging it. But for a short time, as the boat spanked across the lake, her eyes fastened on the horizon without seeing a thing.

To her disappointment, the agent phoned to cancel the meeting. "I'm in the middle of one of those sticky deals," he said. "Racing back and forth with offers and counteroffers, and both parties anxious to close the deal as soon as possible. You're in the business; you must know. I didn't realize this was going to happen, but as it has . . ."

"That's all right," Lacey said. One safe night on the island had made her a little less afraid of the next. "How about tomorrow?"

"Can I phone you? I hate to set up another appointment only to break it again."

She agreed.

And then there was another solitary afternoon on the dock, and some more healing sun, and another healing night. . . .

In many ways it was typical of a number of days that were to come.

Several days passed before the appointment with the real estate agent actually came to pass. By the time it did Lacey was becoming excessively annoyed. One day it rained heavily; he pointed out that a trip would be wasted because he could take no pictures of the cottage. Another day there was a problem with the boat he had arranged to borrow; he claimed he couldn't find another. On a Saturday he was playing in a golf championship. On a Sunday he didn't work, because that was his one day with the family. On a Monday . . .

"If you *really* have to spend all afternoon with another client," Lacey said tartly, "don't bother coming at all. By this time tomorrow I'll have had an appointment with your competition. Either that, or I'll advertise the property myself."

"I'll be there right away," the man said.

She smiled, satisfied. She understood all his excuses, but there came a time when one had to take a stand. There wasn't a great deal of choice in local agents, and this man had an excellent reputation. She knew, because she'd inquired.

After that their business went fairly smoothly. She could not fault his knowledge or his efficiency once he arrived on the scene. He suggested a number of repairs and a coat of paint on the trim, but Lacey pointed out that she couldn't afford those things, and whoever bought would probably tear the whole thing down and build anew, anyway. She gave him the listing with a sigh of relief, for she could now think about returning home.

But the days of delay had had an effect. To her surprise, she realized she no longer felt such urgency about departing. The afternoons of lazing and the nights of sleeping well, without suffering too many unnatural urges, were beginning to drain away some of the poison that ran in the deepest wellsprings of her being.

Having recognized this, she mused about it the next day, during a sun-drenched afternoon she had decided would be her last. Bikini-clad, she lay on the dock, knowing she was safe from Gideon's eyes because only a short time before, she had seen him high in the air, riding the rainbow kite.

It was one of those rare, slow, beautiful Muskoka afternoons when the wind was still and the pine-perfumed air seemed breathless with summer perfection. A pair of dragonflies mated in an elegant aerial pas de deux. A spider spun its delicate web and waited patiently. A myriad minuscule waterbugs skated on the surface of the dark, still lake . . . dispersed when a fish splashed the water . . . reassembled to join in an obscure, complex dance foreordained by nature. The drone of distant boats punctuated the sleepy silence, but only occasionally, for it was mid-week and the lake traffic was minimal.

Lacey felt almost safe. She felt almost at peace. She felt almost whole.

Stretched on the dock, chin propped on her hands, she looked at the linked dragonflies and envied them their lack of human cognition, their absence of morality. But it was a dreamy envy, a wistful wishing that contained no real pain.

A full week had now passed since the night she'd spent in Gideon's arms, and the week had done some healing. While it could not be said that she believed herself pure of heart, she was beginning to feel stronger about herself, more cognizant of the fact that, in the first flush of her young love for Gideon, she herself had been an innocent party, except for the single sin of loving too deeply and too soon.

Once sullied, and in a way that went far, far beyond the expected or the expectable, she had felt physically torn apart. In the dark unspeakable sin that had been unwittingly committed, there was no going back. How could she ever be pure again, once she had lost the symbol of her purity?

The desecration of technical virginity, closely followed by unnatural shame instead of natural passion, had left her with a deep sense of original sin that had turned her exceptionally vulnerable to a second encounter with Gideon. In his presence she had become painfully aware of her sexual weaknesses instead of her moral strengths.

And yet was she really so sexually weak? Surely the past eight years had proved otherwise, except for this last lapse. And what were her moral strengths? She thought she must have some.

She tried to remember a few and managed to make a small list that helped to bolster her self-esteem. All those nights she had felt so pulled, she had not traveled the path that would have led her to Gideon's arms. Nor, during that first week when he was unaware of the relationship, had she consciously tried to encourage or entice him in any way. In fact, the opposite was true. She had dressed carefully, refused invitations, avoided him whenever possible. What had happened had happened, and she couldn't deny responsibility for that . . . but it had been unplanned. And given the intimate circumstances, perhaps she could not have changed her course, any more than the mating dragonflies could alter theirs.

Yes; Lacey was feeling stronger, just as Gideon had predicted. And the slow flow of the days, the rhythm of routine, had fortified her growing confidence.

During the mornings, when she and Gideon usually visited the hospital together, there were no suggestive overtones. She began to recognize that when he made no overtures, her feelings remained in check. Whether he had accepted his mother's part in the past, Lacey was not to know. But at least he had accepted that he ought to direct his amorous attentions elsewhere. The pain of that was balanced by its rightness.

During the afternoons there were no encounters

at all. Gideon spent a good deal of his time with Debbie, Lacey thought. He hadn't told her this was so, and she hadn't asked, for she felt it was none of her business. But nearly every afternoon she saw the rainbow kite soaring high in the sky, and when it carried a man, she didn't need to do much guessing. She had had to squint at first, but by now she recognized the tiny strip of yellow that was Gideon's bathing suit.

During the evenings she read. She had found a few G.J. Llewelyn books around the cottage: Aunt Edwina's prized autographed editions. She had started the first with trepidation, afraid that to read it would only feed her obsession. But soon she had found herself altogether engrossed—incongruously able to forget Gideon himself while occupied in reading his works.

And during the nights she slept. Her dreams were largely untroubled and unerotic. The most disturbing, and it didn't seem so disturbing while she slept, was a recurring dream in which she lay secure in Gideon's platonic embrace, slowly drifting under a tunnel of gloomy overhanging trees, in a rudderless boat that had no paddle. The dream was pervaded with warmth and love, but there was also a profound sadness to it, a sense of forlornness and fatalism because of the inability to change the boat's course. After that dream she would wake feeling melancholy, but peaceful.

Perhaps Gideon had been right in telling her to stay. The unhurried pulse of the lakes and the pace of the long, lazy Muskoka summer were beginning to let some peace seep into her heart, replacing the poison and the pollution of illicit, morally unacceptable thoughts. Time could change nothing, and indeed nothing had changed; but perhaps at some point she could learn to forgive herself for being weak and flawed and human.

The dragonflies skimmed off into the distance, altering their course after all, and Lacey decided to stay in Muskoka a little longer.

Chapter Nine

Time continued to move, each tomorrow gliding smoothly and effortlessly into the present until it became yet another yesterday, like beads being counted on an abacus of slow summer days. A cool spell came and went, a stormy spell came and went, a windy spell came and went, and then for a while there was rain. The whole world was gray with it, and the old cottage grew chilly and damp beneath the incessant drizzle. To prevent mildewy odors, log fires in the great stone fireplace became a daily necessity, and Lacey was glad of the lean-to full of dry cordwood and kindling, stockpiled by Gideon for Aunt Edwina's use.

To stay in Muskoka had been a decision of the heart, not of the head. But with the change of weather, Lacey decided it hadn't been a totally irrational move. During that period the few prospective buyers who arrived to see the Eyrie seemed to chat a lot about restoring, not about ripping down. Perhaps that was because they were mostly local cottagers—it wasn't great weather to attract outsiders. The old place was considerably warmer and more welcoming with a big log fire crackling in the hearth, and Lacey began to feel that her daily presence served some purpose. The talk of renovation spurred her to spend some of the rainy afternoons wallpapering and painting, adding to the cottage's interior charm.

With the finely honed intuition of a professional real estate agent, Lacey recognized that most prospects were merely sightseeing, taking the opportunity to peek into another person's summer home. They had no intention of buying at any price. However, that was true of virtually every real estate transaction and didn't change the fact that the *next* arrival might actually be a serious buyer. With fires, friendly wallpaper, and a little fresh paint, she hoped to add to the cottage's salability.

Offers were slow in coming. Despite the great size of the Eyrie, which justified the price, half a million dollars was far, far beyond the reach of all but the very rich. Lacey herself had eliminated many potential prospects by narrowing the field. She had told the agent to bring only those buyers who appeared to want the island for family purposes, and she had also informed him that she wouldn't consider splitting the ten-acre property in any way.

She suspected one prospect was a speculator, and at that point told the real estate agent that she would entertain no offers unless they contained a clause guaranteeing that the land would not be divided for at least ten years. No offer came.

She received a sizable check from Pittsburgh, her share of the commission on a property for which she had brought in the listing some months before. It arrived like manna from heaven, just at a point when she had been wondering if she'd made a mistake in staying in Muskoka. It paid the ongoing expenses of her father's care and gave her enough to get by for the rest of the summer, with a small amount to spare. With a sense of wonderment, she realized that she had reached a decision without even being aware of it. She *did* intend to stay for the rest of the summer.

Having realized that, she had her own phone installed. It was still a party line, but not the same line as Gideon's. Debbie Halloran had called him a few times, and Lacey preferred not to know about it.

The check by no means provided solutions for everything. There was still the problem of what to do about the marina bill. For a time she avoided Hobie Hubbard during her trips into town. He had phoned to say that one of her boats, the big Ditchburn, was usable if she wanted to pick it up. "She ain't spit an' polish," he said, "but she's the best I kin do, without some mighty major work. Like you said, I stopped. At least, soon's I could. That ole battery, I recharged it. Save you the price of a new one. Should do you for this summer, Miz Lacey, though I ain't making promises. Mebbe she will, mebbe she won't." By now Hobie was well aware that the Wynward fortune was not as Aunt Edwina had depicted. With no reason to support her aunt's foolish pretenses in future, Lacey had told him the truth.

At first she was evasive about when she would

pick up the boat. Not wanting to be dependent on Gideon, she would have liked the transportation; but she felt she couldn't take delivery of the big Ditchburn without paying the bill. By now it was a considerable sum that she couldn't hope to pay off until she received the proceeds from the island. As the boats were to be sold with the Eyrie, a part of the total price, it would have been best to have them all on hand, but that simply wasn't possible.

When Hobie began to grow fretful, unhappy to have the thirty-foot launch cluttering up the limited boathouse space in the marina, she finally struck a deal with him. The unusual old disappearing-propeller boat, though not so very much bigger than a large rowboat and totally inoperable at the moment, was an extremely valuable antique with a ready market. Hobie sold it for her. The selling price more than covered his bill, and Lacey recovered her Ditchburn with money in pocket. With more sadness than she would have thought possible, she went into Hobie's workshop for a last nostalgic farewell to the dilapidated, obsolete, lovely little Dippy, reminding herself that at least it would be restored to its old beauty under a new owner.

The big mahogany boat was still skittish, and the battery was definitely sluggish. Gideon insisted on continuing his chauffeur service. "I'd be visiting your aunt anyway," he said. Lacey gave in without too much demur. Her deepest feelings for Gideon would never really alter, but he was not the threat he had once been. No longer so self-destructive in her emotions, she hadn't sat in the casement window for many, many nights.

Aunt Edwina continued to hover between life

and death. Lacey no longer felt the necessity of daily visits, which had become something of a burden since the moment of recognizing the anger she had been suppressing for so many years. It was a long round trip, nearly two hours including the time spent in the hospital, and didn't serve much purpose when Aunt Edwina never recognized her anyway. Lacey told Gideon she intended to go only every second day, then changed it to every third.

She thought he would be glad of the opportunity to return to his morning writing schedule. Instead, to her surprise, she discovered some days later that he had gone to the hospital alone on those occasions when she hadn't.

She learned of his visits inadvertently from the nurse, Gladdie Brenner, during a rainy-day trip to Bracebridge. On the return trip home she questioned Gideon about it, waiting until they were in his boat because she was curious to see his expression when he answered.

She turned toward him once the boat was out in the lake. She hoped, no, *knew*, that her reasons for wanting to see Gideon's face were not what they had been of old. All the same, it moved her to look directly at him, for she usually avoided it. And so it took her a moment to adjust her thinking and remember her question. The summer of sun had at last bronzed Gideon's hair as it used to do, bleaching and streaking the exposed surfaces so that by daylight and at first glance he almost appeared to be a coppery blond. Lacey knew that when he ran his fingers through his hair, the underpelt of dark brown was still there.

At last she formulated her words, questioning the purpose of his daily visits to the hospital.

Gideon shrugged away her curiosity. "For some ridiculous reason, I'm attached to the old lady. Besides, I have other reasons for driving into Bracebridge."

"Oh? I thought your alter ego liked to write in the mornings."

"I'm not writing now, I'm researching. Going through old newspaper archives. G.J. Llewelyn doesn't invent all those historical facts he throws around, you know."

After a little pause Lacey said, "I've been reading some of your books, Gideon." She felt oddly hesitant about broaching the subject, and this was the first time she had done so. She added sincerely, "I'm impressed, and not in the same way I was before. They take me right out of myself."

"I'm glad," he said gravely. "That's a fine compliment."

Her throat hurt because she loved him too much. But her eyes had learned discipline, and so she turned them forward, not looking at him again during the rest of the approach to the Eyrie.

Later she thought about the conversation. Gideon might have ample reason for undertaking his long daily journey; nevertheless, Lacey knew he could have searched the newspaper archives without visiting the hospital. He might be fond of her aunt, but it was above and beyond the call of duty to visit an old lady every single day, especially as she was daily sinking further into senility and now seldom recognized even Gideon.

Lacey had wanted to watch his face because it had occurred to her that he must still be hoping for some moments of lucidity in order to question Aunt Edwina about the past. Had Gideon still not accepted his mother's lapse from grace, then? Lacey had to wonder, but would never put the question to him directly. She and he no longer discussed such intimate matters. Though always wary and aware in each other's presence—Lacey was, at least—they had fallen into a reasonably comfortable and companionable pattern, and she didn't like to disrupt it by injecting the wrong thoughts. To bring up the incestuous past was to walk a dangerous path, strewn with the deep and fatal traps of dark, elemental emotions.

Gideon was avoiding that path, and so was she. She never inquired about his doings, nor he about hers. He had taken to parking his boat at his own end of the island, and she had taken to doing her own cottage repairs, at least those she was capable of, so she wouldn't have to ask him for help. They virtually never connected, except during trips to the hospital.

Good weather, hot lake weather, returned at last. More prospective buyers saw the cottage, and Lacey turned down two serious offers because they were too low. Not so very long before, she would have accepted either one of them with gratitude and relief. But common sense had returned along with growing personal peace, and she knew she could do far better if she waited. She began to think it wasn't so important to sell this year.

Sunshine sent the rainbow kite and its lean bronzed rider back into the sky. Lacey didn't even trouble to squint to see the color of the man's hair. The abacus of time counted on. With August, the days began to shorten. Queen Anne's lace feathered into delicate gray-white profusion along the roadsides on the mainland, replacing other wildflowers. The blueberries on the Eyrie's rockiest point were ripe. Fresh, local corn on the cob arrived in the stores, and everyone rejoiced. Debbie phoned and invited Lacey to use the sauna one afternoon, but she declined on some pretext or another. Hobie's wife sprained her wrist. And the beads of time kept sliding from future to past, and all the little happenings were the colors of the beads.

In the slow slide of the days, Lacey continued to mend without even being aware of it.

She flew back to Pittsburgh for a few days, made one property sale while she was there, and returned to Muskoka feeling relatively flush with success. She arranged to have the old canoe not just caulked but refinished, and got a price on shoring up the casement projection at some future date. The Hallorans had another party, a communal corn roast, the same week she was away, and Lacey begged off for good and sufficient reason. One of the Halloran children got chicken pox— shades of Lacey's seventeenth summer!—then a second, then a third. The Ditchburn sprung a bad leak, and Lacey didn't dare ask Hobie to investigate the reason. Instead, she took to running the bilge pump both morning and night. She squirmed her way out of a second invitation to use the sauna. Another neighbor invited her in for drinks, and she accepted. She wallpapered two more rooms, thought about painting the kitchen or even the outside trim on the cottage, and decided it was nicer to lie on the dock in the afternoon sun.

The August days were dwindling and she wanted to enjoy them.

She received another bid on the island. The gap

between asking price and offering price was much narrower, but the customers, a prosperous lawyer and his wife, had arrived with an architect. With faint distaste on their faces, they had talked about ripping down the old cottage and the old boathouse and building something large, clean, modern, and, from the sound of it, vastly expensive. They specifically excluded the Ditchburn and the cottage contents in their offer, because they didn't want the bother of getting rid of them.

Lacey thought about her newly wallpapered rooms and the cheerful curtains she'd made for the kitchen. She thought about the boathouse window boxes, now planted with bright geraniums. She thought about the old stone fireplace and the trouble she'd gone to, cleaning its smoke-blackened mantel. She thought about the antique bentwood chair she'd stripped. She thought about the furniture slipcovers she'd made so long ago; they looked almost new since they'd been freshened with a wash. She thought about the sagging casement window and the mournful moosehead. She thought about the big mahogany boat, its eccentricities, its unrestored top, its unrepaired bottom, its thirst for love as well as money. With a rashness no businesswoman should ever show, she didn't even bother to sign back the offer, at any price. She told the agent not to bring more offers from the same couple.

And so the days passed, and so the healing went on. By the end of August, when the slant of the sun laid long tree shadows over the boathouse by the hour of suppertime, Lacey began to wonder if she would ever want to go. But she knew she must, and soon.

The Hallorans issued an invitation to a final roundup, last party of the season, planned for Friday of the Labor Day weekend. Lacey accepted, guiltily conscious that she had avoided them far too much over the summer. It was because of Gideon, of course. She hadn't wanted to see him with Debbie.

"Next year," she found herself saying to Mrs. Halloran, greatly to her own surprise, "next year, when the cottage is fixed up, maybe I'll manage to do a little entertaining myself."

If she hadn't heard herself say it, she would not have believed she could have such a thought. Well, why not? By next year there would be no reason to see Gideon at all, because Aunt Edwina wouldn't linger forever. And the odd time she did run into him—well, with another year of Muskoka, she might actually work up some immunity. Lacey felt she could cope with her feelings about him now, certainly better than she had. And even though he had refused to buy the island himself, she didn't really want to sell it out from under him.

With calm acceptance of a decision that made not a single scrap of sense, she phoned the real estate agent and told him she was taking the island off the market.

That did bring Gideon around, when he saw that the For Sale signs had gone down. He arrived in late afternoon, the day of the Hallorans' party. The glorious weather had turned into an end-of-season heat wave. A blast-furnace sun caused distorted shimmerings on the surface of the lake. Though the sky was clear, the air was close and heavy and would probably remain so until rinsed by rain.

Lacey was smoothing suntan lotion over her shoulders, bikini straps lowered, when the orange boat swooped in to her dock. For a few vital seconds the dramatic landing surprised her into forgetting her dangling straps. Only half an hour before, she had seen the rainbow kite in the sky, first carrying Debbie, then carrying Gideon. She would not have expected him to be back in his own boat quite so soon.

Gideon's eyes flicked at her shoulders but didn't linger there. He smiled, his manner casual and faintly detached, as usual calculated to set her at her ease. "Mind if I drop by?"

"You already have," she pointed out, and the habit of a less volcanic relationship allowed her answering smile to appear quite genuine. But she was bothered by his arrival, more than she would allow herself to show.

Unhurriedly, so as not to draw attention to them, she pushed the straps back in place. She made a useless wish about the size of the scraps of black cloth covering her, and another about the absence of her beach coat. The customary privacy she had enjoyed for weeks, along with the unclouded sky and the excessive heat of the weather, had lulled her into leaving it elsewhere. She thought about the big beach towel she had spread out to lie on, but decided that to wrap herself in that right after applying suntan lotion would be far too obvious, betraying a frame of mind she oughtn't to be in. Besides, it was too hot for such coverings to be justified.

"I'd like to invite myself in for a drink," Gideon said offhandedly. "I've even brought the where-withal, a thermos flask full of sangria I prepared for the occasion. And two glasses. Permission to come ashore?"

There was only the tiniest pause before Lacey said, "Of course. Granted."

As Gideon stepped out on the dock, she saw that he was wearing an old T-shirt and a pair of trim bathing trunks. His long muscled legs were mahogany-colored from a whole summer's sun, the dusting of hair on them bleached so that it now vanished into the tan. His feet were bare, too, something that had disturbed her deeply once before. She was enormously aware of his physical impact, and although her limbs hadn't quite turned to custard, she found she was shaky in a way she had thought she'd put behind her.

While he tied up to the boat rings, Lacey shook her hair forward so that it spilled over her breasts, partially curtaining the cleavage. The hair was thick, and a great deal longer after two months of not being cut. It did a creditable job of concealment.

Gideon found two ancient canvas deck chairs inside the boathouse. Having wisely checked them for safety, he set them up and positioned two big plastic tumblers and a wide-mouthed thermos flask between them on the dock. Lacey waited until he was bent over pouring drinks and then slipped into one of the chairs, her beach towel now casually draped over her lap.

Straightening, Gideon handed her a glass and kept one for himself. Sliver-thin slices of orange and lemon floated in the sangria, a cooling punch of red wine and fruit juice. It was the perfect drink for a blazing day, thirst-quenching, aesthetically appealing, and not too strong.

"You've taken the Eyrie off the market, I see."

"Yes."

"Unsold, too, I hear." He raised his tumbler. "Shall we drink a toast to that?"

"A toast? Because it's unsold?"

"On the contrary. Because it's sold," he said calmly, reaching forward to touch his glass to hers. "I hope you're still prepared to accept my offer? I'm having it put back into writing."

Lacey's jaw dropped; she couldn't help it. Dumbfounded, she stared, licked her lips, stared some more, nervously pushed her hair back without remembering why she had left it dangling over her breasts in the first place, and then continued staring "I don't know," she said at last, slowly. "I'll have to think about it."

Gideon seemed unperturbed by her lack of enthusiasm. He sipped at his sangria, watching her with shuttered eyes and an air of faint amusement. "May I ask why you took it off the market? Could it be that you're planning to return and use it yourself next summer? I hear you've been doing a lot of fixing up."

"That was to . . . to help sell it."

"But you didn't sell. Are you holding on out of the goodness of your heart, so I won't have to move?"

"I wouldn't do that!"

"Why not? You did it for your aunt Edwina."

Lacey steadied herself. "That was a different matter altogether. If you planned to buy all along, why did you withdraw your offer in the first place? I've been wondering all summer."

"No guesses?"

"I . . . no, not really. At first, when I was angry,

I thought it was because you wanted to bring me down to a *really* low price. I thought I shouldn't have told you I was so desperate. I expected you'd come back with a low bid in a week or two, when my cash had run out."

"Did you really think that?"

Lacey sighed. "No, not really. At least, not for long. It didn't seem like you. Besides, when the weeks slid by and you didn't appear with an offer, it didn't make a whole lot of sense."

"No other guesses?"

"Well, I . . . for a little time I thought maybe you were considering moving right off the Eyrie. I mean, I thought you might decide you didn't need the island if . . ."

"If what?"

Lacey felt her cheeks growing dusky with color, as if she had been a young girl. Her eyes escaped into contemplation of Gideon's boat. She began to rock it with a naked toe, so she could watch it bob up and down at dockside. "Well, Debbie has her own little cabin over at the Hallorans', doesn't she?" Her tone was somewhat defiant. "Actually, I had the notion that you might have moved right into it. Whenever the Eyrie was being shown, I used to phone the bunkhouse to warn you that someone was coming. You were never there, even in early morning. After a while I began to wonder if you were living somewhere else altogether."

"I have been rather busy this summer," he said dryly. "I admit I haven't spent much time on the Eyrie, but why on earth would you think I'd want to move off altogether?"

She bit her lip because she didn't want to point out the answer to that a second time. It would sound as though she was asking him to deny—or confirm—his relationship with Debbie. And Lacey didn't need confirmation. The evening she'd had drinks on a neighboring island, some chance remark, rather disparaging to Debbie, had touched on the liaison with Gideon. "A good-time girl," the gossipy hostess had called her, when her husband went off to fix drinks. "Even though she was involved with Gideon all last summer—and the summer before—she actually used to flirt with my husband. Imagine that, when all the time she was sleeping with another man! When I found her trying to drag Aubrey into the sauna this summer, that was the last straw. We stopped seeing the Hallorans altogether." Jealousy had played a part in that particular revelation, but that hadn't made it any the less telling. It only reaffirmed what Lacey already knew. She thought it a sure thing that Gideon's affair with Debbie had continued. Over the course of the summer there had been more than enough clues that they were still seeing each other.

Gideon pressed for a response. "How would it make sense for me to move off the island, when I've gone to a great deal of trouble to fit the bunkhouse up as a work studio? And when I've been wanting to own the place for years?"

"It doesn't, really," Lacey confessed with a sigh. "Anyway, Gideon, I tried not to do all that much thinking about the whole thing. You had decided not to buy, and that was that. I finally decided it was just as you said, none of my business."

"Why do you think I want to buy *now?*"

She realized that the rocking action of her foot had stopped. She resumed it, paying rapt attention to her own bare toes. "I suppose," she said with a total lack of inflection, "you've decided it's safer."

"Safer?"

"Er . . . at this point I have to assume that you really *do* want the island. And if you don't own it, well . . . I might sell it at any time, or I might kick you off without warning. And that's not safe, is it?"

"No, it's not, is it?" he echoed affably.

A much larger toe suddenly appeared not very far from her own and joined in the rhythmic swinging motion. Lacey's foot snapped back to the vicinity of her chair. She glanced up at Gideon. His face was bland, but she could almost swear it had changed in that very moment. She had a subliminal impression of a wide grin being wiped away in the instant that she looked up. Feeling as if he and his foot were mocking her in some way, she suddenly grew angry.

"I might not sell to you," she said, her tone quite injured.

"So be it," Gideon said. He shrugged and took a slow, deep swallow of his sangria. His eyes flickered at her, mockery glinting somewhere in their depths. "You can let me know when you decide."

There followed a silence that was awkward for Lacey, but apparently not for Gideon. He continued to rock the boat absently and sip at the sangria while he mused over matters he chose to keep to himself.

After a while he said lazily, "With your gift for ascribing strange motives to me, I imagine you may be wondering whether I'll keep you off the island in future if I do buy. So, just in case a crazy notion like that hits you, I'll tell you that if you ever *do* decide to sell, you're welcome to use this cottage at any time."

Lacey looked up, softening, feeling a rush of warm gratitude. "Thank you," she said simply, but already she knew she would never return if she sold the Eyrie to him. That would change the complexion of the relationship, give him the freedom of the island, rob her of some of the ability to control how much she saw of him.

"I think I'd better give you a list of my other motives, too, for it seems you're very bad at guessing. When I withdrew my offer, it was simply in order to force you to stay. To be frank, my friend at the real estate office gave me a little help in the matter."

"To force me to stay . . ." She looked at him as realization struck, feeling as if her mind must have been benumbed for weeks. Of course! Why had it never occurred to her before? The real estate agent . . . the delays . . . the excuses . . .

And by the time a week had passed, the worst of Lacey's desperation was over; she had no longer needed to run.

Gideon's mouth had turned sober and serious, and now he didn't look as though he was deriding her in any way. "If you had been able to make an instant sale at that point, Lacey, you would have run—and you'd have spent the rest of your life thinking of yourself as the kind of person you're not. I thought if you stayed, you'd begin to understand yourself a little better."

At length her eyes dropped, unable to meet his. "Thank you for that too," she said. And she meant it, even though at this particular moment, with her mind misbehaving more than it had done for some time, she was not sure she ought to have been congratulating herself on having any moral fiber at all. The peace of the past few weeks seemed remarkably elusive.

"It was a bit of a gamble, of course. You might have sold the property to someone else. I would have restored my offer much sooner, but when I heard you were putting on restrictions . . . well, at that point I decided to have faith. I knew there wouldn't be a whole lot of action at the price you were asking."

Gideon hadn't left everything to chance, although he wasn't going to tell that to Lacey. Real estate agents were supposed to work for the seller, so Gideon hadn't been given any hard information, facts or figures, but he had been promised a warning in the event that an acceptance seemed imminent. Some days earlier he'd learned that an excellent offer was in, and it was at that point that his renewed bid for the property had been prepared. It hadn't been needed after all, so Gideon had given instructions to hold it. And then, when Lacey had taken the Eyrie off the market, he had told the agent that he would prefer to present the proposition to her personally and informally. One way or another, the agent would get his fee for services rendered.

And there had been another small persuasion, too, which he hoped Lacey would never discover. On the day she'd been most desperate to run, he had suspected that she might call the marina for transportation. He'd spoken to Hobie Hubbard and dropped a number of hints that the bill for

Ditchburn repairs might never be paid without pressure. When Lacey had called for a launch to pick her up, he'd been standing there in the shop. Hobie had obliged by pressing for payment, and Lacey had obliged by withdrawing her request. Gideon had been grimly satisfied.

Instinctively, he had known that Lacey shouldn't run. During the night of revelation, a night burned into Gideon's brain, Lacey's tears had touched him profoundly. He had seen her torn conscience, her despair, her burden of shame and deep, deep guilt. With knowledge of her inner battles to guide him, many things had begun to come clear. Years before, he had taken her virginity; he knew that. He had a responsibility to help her understand that her sins, if any, were human and few.

During the weeks that followed, he had only been able to hope that she wouldn't run away from the situation. He felt that if he left her strictly alone, she would at some point come to recognize that she hadn't actually made sexual overtures to him, that she had only given in to circumstance and the unbearable pressures of confused emotions, a naturally passionate nature, and the unnatural shame of an old, heavy guilt she had mistakenly been trying to carry alone. Believing that she had already committed an unforgivable sin against nature, she had been left vulnerable to commit another—or so Gideon had come to comprehend. He couldn't watch her movements at every moment, and so he had been on tenterhooks for some time, his only surety her lack of marine transportation, which had ended when she paid Hobie's bill.

He thought the summer had helped her. Her

eyes were no longer dark with sleeplessness, and for the most part she was easier in his presence. Her conscience ought not to be so troubled, he reflected: she tried hard enough to hide herself when he was around. He was half amused to see that the long licorice-black tresses had found their way back over her breasts, and the towel so artlessly draped on her lap had a purpose that Gideon recognized very well. If she thought herself sinful at the moment, it was most certainly all in her head.

Lacey was ignorant of all of Gideon's machinations over the course of the summer. "What would you have done if I *had* sold to someone else?"

"Gone back home, sadder but a helluva lot wiser. Or rather, wiser but a helluva lot sadder."

"Home?"

"I do exist the rest of the time, you know—not just during the months I'm in Muskoka. I spend eight, nine months of every year in the Poconos. I have a log cabin there, on a heavily wooded slope. It's a bit of an antique, just like this cottage, except it's been restored." Lacey didn't grab the conversational ball, so he continued with his description. " 'Cabin' doesn't describe it too well, for it's quite large. Several bedrooms, big friendly kitchen, living room with a fantastic view, fireplaces practically wall-to-wall in nearly every room, a study in the treetops. I have a housekeeper there; I do like to be pampered for part of the year. Oh—and a great big hot tub. Does it all fill you with envy?"

"It sounds very nice," Lacey said. She was staring at his foot as if its movements mesmerized her. And indeed they did, and so did the tight, taut curve of his muscled calf, and so did the clean bend of his knee . . . oh, God, was it going to start all over again? Mention of the hot tub hadn't helped. The hair at the nape of her neck was prickling.

She dragged her eyes away. "I've decided to sell you the Eyrie, Gideon. Can we settle it tomorrow?"

Gideon refreshed the drinks from the chilled, swirling contents of his thermos. "How about tonight?"

"There's the Hallorans' party," she reminded him. "It starts very soon. Debbie would be upset if you didn't go."

"Oh, damn." Gideon scowled briefly, and then his face became enigmatic again, thoughts hidden behind lowered eyes. "Well, I'd be prepared to disappoint Debbie and the whole crowd of her friends, just in order to get this settled once and for all. Tell you what, I'll feed you tonight—I have a few frozen casseroles at the bunkhouse. Hobie's wife supplies them for me regularly, and she's a great cook. We'll have a quiet dinner, talk over the details. Well? How about it?"

She could feel the damp heat start, centering in the skin shielded by the drape of the beach towel. "I couldn't possibly miss the party."

"We could always go for the end of it . . . if you're still in the mood, that is. This thing is pretty damn important to me, Lacey. I've been wanting to own the Eyrie for years."

There was nothing at all suggestive in his manner, and yet his very persuasiveness unsettled her. "There's nothing much to talk over. The Eyrie is yours if you want it."

Gideon laughed. "There's a little matter of money. How do you know I'm going to make the same offer?"

"Aren't you?"

"Not exactly. Well, Lacey? Dinner?"

"That's not necessary. I can settle everything with your agent."

"There are a few other things we should talk over, not just the offer. Personal things that have nothing to do with the business arrangement. If we're going to continue sharing this island in the future, there are details we ought to decide. We should think about renovations to be done to the cottage, use of the boathouse, use of the boats—"

"No!" She was beginning to feel panicky. "There's nothing to talk about, Gideon, because I'm not coming back to the Eyrie next year. You'll have the property all to yourself."

"Not coming *back?*" Gideon was instantly alert, his whole body tensing. "But—"

Lacey rose to her feet, draping the towel over her shoulders in the same swift movement. "I think you'd better go now, Gideon. As far as your offer's concerned, there's nothing to talk about. I accept your terms, whatever they are. I'll go to your agent's office tomorrow morning and settle everything then and there, before I leave."

Gideon was on his feet, too, his eyes cutting into her with sudden anger. "Leave? For Pittsburgh? You can't do that!"

"But I am." It was an instant decision, made at that very moment. She could not have said exactly why it had suddenly become important again, but it had. She would pack up and go first thing in the morning, pay one last visit to Aunt Edwina along the way, and then drive directly to the States. She retreated along the dock by a few feet. The dark shadow of a tree fell on her, reminding her that she had a very good excuse for getting away. "Look, Gideon, I've got to go. I have to get dressed for the Hallorans' party—it must be about to start."

Gideon began to follow, but in his haste he knocked over the half-filled thermos and the deck chair Lacey had been using. The thermos rolled beneath his foot, throwing him off balance, and the deck chair collapsed in an ungainly heap, a second obstacle to his progress along the dock.

Lacey was fast vanishing. As he tried to untangle his feet from the deck chair, he called after her. "For God's sake, Lacey, I've *got* to talk to you! I have things to tell you! Dammit, I've spent the whole summer looking into this—morning, noon, and night, asking questions all over the lake! Listening to people reminisce! Going into old newspaper files! Dammit, Lacey, the least you can do is listen! I think you were wrong about my mother!"

Lacey's dash to the cottage was nearly complete. So she was right—Gideon still hadn't accepted. But she had, and nothing he could say would ever explain away that snapshot she had found in her father's desk. The smile, the dimpled cheek, the gazebo in the background. And the hastily scribbled note that had been found in the envelope with it, along with the other mementos of Peggy Llewelyn: *I'm pregnant, Jacob. What shall I do? Peggy.*

"We've got to talk!" Gideon thundered.

Lacey turned for a final glance at him. She called

back, "Then you'll have to talk to me at the Hallorans' party, Gideon, for I refuse to talk to you anywhere else. Now if you'll please leave—this is still my property, and I'm ordering you to get off!"

She entered the cottage and locked it with one of the many bolts installed weeks before.

Chapter Ten

$\mathcal{G}$ideon spent some minutes rattling at the various doors of the cottage, cursing vehemently, trying to get in. At last, watching covertly from a window, Lacey saw him leap into his boat with a savage expression on his face. He took off at a roar, the backwash of his departure creating waves high enough to force a spray of water up through the narrow gaps in the plank dock.

The rattling of doors was only the last of the things to upset her, and as soon as Gideon was out of sight, Lacey tried to sort out her distressingly tangled thoughts. She had been very perturbed by the encounter, perhaps more than circumstances had at first warranted. She'd already suspected that Gideon might be hoping to clear his mother, so that was not the only cause for her disturbance. She had started to feel shaky long before the mention of Peggy Llewelyn. And why . . . ? Was it the discovery that Gideon had conspired to have her stay in Muskoka? The faint gleam in his eye? The toe joining hers at the edge of the boat? The invitation to dinner? The mention of sharing the island next year?

And then it suddenly came to her, in a blinding flash, that one of the things that had disturbed her throughout the encounter was Gideon's bathing suit. She had avoided looking directly at it, but she had been aware of it, as she was aware of every part and particle of him. As she saw those trim trunks again in her mind's eye, a little doubt pricked at her, and the doubt began to grow.

With a haste that could only be warranted by sudden fear, she ran outside to a high point of land that gave a good overview of a great sweep of the lake. The rainbow kite was still up in the sky. She squinted until she could see the sex of the rider and the narrow strip of his bathing suit. The man on the kite wore yellow, as he had done all summer. And Gideon's bathing trunks were navy blue.

That wasn't Gideon with Debbie Halloran; it hadn't been all summer. Instead, Gideon had been asking questions around the lake, trying to convince himself that he wasn't Lacey's brother. And after that dinner invitation and the passionate rattling of the doors, she had the strong feeling that his mother's moral code was not the only thing at stake. Gideon hadn't been involved with Debbie, and he still wanted *her*.

The thought set Lacey's knees to trembling. If Gideon had convinced himself that he wasn't her brother, he had become an immense threat. He would have no reason to avoid touching her. It suffocated Lacey to think of the protestations he might make, the physical blandishments he might choose to use. . . .

She didn't want to hear anything he had to say; it could only lead to more distress. But if he absolutely insisted on talking—yes, she would listen. But she wouldn't listen in private, only in the ambience of the Hallorans' party, as she had said. There was safety to be found in numbers.

She threw on some clothes, hardly conscious of her choice, and left for the Hallorans' at once. She was still very shaky when she reached their island in her revitalized canoe. She was the first to arrive. She had been there for a good fifteen minutes before a second guest arrived, and after that the crowd gradually grew.

Debbie arrived at the dock with a young man who didn't look at all like Gideon—except in the vaguest way, due to his muscular build. His hair was mid-brown, not burnished by the sun like Gideon's, but it was weeks since Lacey had tried to determine the color of the kite-skier's hair. Earlier, Gideon's hair had been mid-brown too. It confirmed to Lacey that all month she had been watching the movements of the wrong man.

As Debbie emerged onto the dock, she waved gaily at Lacey, unaware of the reason for her guest's stricken stare. "Hi, stranger! Long time no see!" Throughout the evening to come, Debbie and her man friend were often seen together, their arms linked with easy, intimate familiarity.

Lacey was trying to lose herself in idle chatter with a host already three sheets to the wind, when she glanced down and saw that she'd worn one white sandal and one navy blue. She solved the problem by slipping them both off and depositing them in her canoe. She didn't want to go back to the cottage. In her present frame of mind, she had the unsettling feeling that Gideon might be over there with a crowbar. He was on the Eyrie, she knew. The orange boat was tied up at his dock—she could see it across the channel between the islands—but he still hadn't turned up at the party.

The end-of-season gathering was not quite as large as the Hallorans' island-warming had been, but the arrangements were more or less the same. The flowing drinks, the excited children, the easy camaraderie, the long buffet table set up outdoors to receive the provisions of the coming barbecue.

More guests came, the food came, dusk came. The children went off for their night of tenting, leaving the adults free to get down to some serious drinking and dancing. The dim lawn lights burned and the music turned romantic. The heat was intense despite the hour, and most of the guests chose not to dance.

"Sauna?" someone suggested.

"Good God, no." It was Debbie. "Who needs a sauna on a night like this?"

"Storm brewing," a man remarked.

Debbie bounced into action. "Well then," she cried, "if we're going to get wet anyway, let's go for a skinny dip! Come on, folks! Everyone for a swim!"

That started a general exodus to the lake. The emptied dance floor and the emptied cottage testified to the intensity of the heat. Most guests, it appeared, had had the foresight to bring bathing suits with them—only a few were following Debbie's suggestion. However, with or without coverings, there was a good deal of splashing and squealing down in the dark, night-shrouded lake.

And still no Gideon. Lacey, who alone of all those at the party had chosen not to swim, began to wonder what she would do at the end of the evening if he didn't turn up. It might mean he was waiting for her at the cottage . . . and how could she return there in the night, in the dark, not knowing what dangers lurked?

It chilled her to think of what might happen if she failed to talk to him here, now, before she left the Hallorans' place. Not so long ago desperate to escape him, she had become exceedingly anxious for his arrival.

Lacey stayed on the patio at some distance from the dock, satisfied to have her presence forgotten. She had pulled her lawn chair back into a deeply shadowed place in order not to draw attention to the fact that she hadn't joined in the general splashing. She had no bathing suit. Her shorts and the loose blouse she wore, a cool tent of a top in light hand-embroidered cotton, had been designed for weather like this, but even so they clung to her heat-dampened skin. She half envied those who felt they could plunge into the lake without clothes, but knew she never would, certainly not when Gideon might arrive on the scene at any moment.

She listened to the splashing and the merry voices. Only a few gleams of the bathers could be seen, and those from the illumination of the lawn lights and the one lamp standard near the dock.

There was no moon at all, and few stars were showing. The night sky, Lacey thought, must be growing heavily overcast.

"Booze cruise?" a slurred male voice called out from the darkness down at the dock. It was Debbie's brother, their host.

"Great idea!"

"Think the storm will break?"

"Nah . . . not yet. Still the odd star up there. Come one, grab your clothes, everyone, let's go. Two boats, eh?"

Lacey had never heard of a booze cruise before, but it didn't take much imagination to interpret the suggestion. She didn't care to go on it—if Gideon arrived, she didn't want to miss him. And yet she didn't wish to remain there alone. She sat tensely, unsure of what to do, hoping against hope that at least a few others would spurn the suggestion.

The merry-makers started to reassemble themselves for the next phase of entertainment. Lacey could hear their talk, see their dim shapes moving through the night. Some climbed into a large boat tied down at the dock, while others began to string along the shore on the path that led to the boathouse.

The host reeled past the patio in search of liquid refreshments, not noticing Lacey in the shadows. At last the arrangements were complete. The boat at the dock took off, running lights lit, a powerful searchlight temporarily switched on to illuminate the dangers in the channel. By its beam, Lacey saw Gideon's orange boat, still parked over at the Eyrie.

Soon another powerful engine could be heard rumbling into life in the well-lit boathouse farther along the shore. At least one other person hadn't joined the party, for Lacey could see a dark silhouette still down at the Hallorans' dock. She sagged with relief.

And then the silhouette moved, and the dim lights glanced over sun-burnished hair, and she saw that it was Gideon. A moment of extreme tension was followed by a stern reminder to herself. At least it was better to see him here, in the relative safety of neutral territory. And perhaps, after all, it was better if nobody was around, for she suspected that the clash between them might be dangerously emotional.

He came up toward the patio, looking for her. He still wore the dark blue bathing suit. How had he arrived without his boat? Had he swum the channel? Lacey had to wonder if he had been at the Hallorans' island for some time, swimming down in the dark with the other bathers, perhaps looking for her. Moisture gleamed over his deep tan and slicked his hair, and the expression on his face was lethally determined.

She rose, moved into his line of vision, and raised a hand to stay him. "Don't come any closer, Gideon. If you want to talk, we'll talk—but I don't want any dramatics."

He had grown very still at the moment of seeing her, and his tense expression had eased. "I thought you must be around somewhere."

Still a little unbalanced by his unexpected arrival, Lacey asked, "How did you get here?"

"I decided to swim over when I saw everyone in the water. I thought if I could find you, it might be a good time to take you aside for a talk, while all the others were occupied. I was damned if I wanted to discuss anything so private in the midst of a noisy, drunken party. I couldn't find you with the swimmers, and I didn't see you go off on the cruise. But I saw your canoe, so I knew you must still be here."

Her voice was slightly shaky as she asked, "What do you want to talk to me about?"

"Surely you know. Lacey . . . I'm not your brother. *I am not your brother*. I'm damn near sure of it now. It's taken me all summer to hunt up the clues, and there are just too many little—"

"Damn *near* sure, Gideon?" she cried. Her knees felt like jelly to hear it put into words, even though it was only a confirmation of what he had implied a short time ago. "That's not good enough," she added. The statement was calmer than her initial cry, but still betrayed some of the tragic hopelessness of her emotions.

With an effort, Gideon kept his voice level and reasonable. "I'll try and go through this quickly. To begin with, there's a good reason your father would have had my mother's photograph. He once made a big play for her—I discovered that. The first clue came at a marina the Llewelyns used to use. Your father used to take the Ditchburn in there for gas when he visited the Llewelyns' island. The owner of the marina remembered the boat, knew it belonged to the Wynwards. He didn't recall the exact year those visits took place, but he remembered that it was exceptionally rainy, because the canvas top was nearly always in use. I checked into that too—and the rainy year was two years before the summer in question, the summer when you say my mother had the affair."

"And *that's* supposed to prove something?"

"Not by itself, but there's more. I talked to a woman who was around back then—a friend of the Llewelyns'—and according to her, my mother didn't give your father the time of day, except as a casual friend. She thinks he actually proposed and my mother turned him down. If he'd once been in love with her, wouldn't that account for him saving mementos? Being a little upset when you asked if I was his son?"

"Gideon, this is pure speculation—"

"And that's not all," he broke in. "I think *my* father may have been in Muskoka during the summer in question. In one of the local newspapers, I ran into a collection of photographs taken during a regatta that summer. There were two young men with a sailboat. No cutlines, and the photograph was a little fuzzy due to poor reproduction, but one of the men could have been my father. And I think the other man was *your* father. At one point your father did own a similar sailboat —I checked into that too. If you were to look at the newspaper—"

"I don't want to hear any of this!" Lacey clasped her hands over her ears, trembling because it was just as she had suspected. Tiny clues, trivial clues— and they meant nothing. Not compared to that snapshot in her father's drawer, not compared to that envelope of mementos, not compared to that note.

Gideon closed the distance and forcibly dragged her hands from their lodging place. His voice became intense, fierce with the need to convince her, and his fingers bit into her wrists. "Lacey! You must listen. Dammit, after all the work I've gone to, can't you give me the benefit of that?"

He stopped and forced himself to ease his brutal grip, struggling for a reasonableness he didn't feel. Still, his voice was fierce with the need to make her listen. "It's damn difficult to find evidence of something that happened three decades ago—especially something that didn't happen out in the full light of day. Do you expect me to turn up with signed confessions from people long dead and gone? With eyewitnesses to an act that nobody would have seen? Thank God I'm accustomed to intensive historical research or I'd have given up long ago! I've gone through dozens of old scrapbooks, photograph albums, newspaper files . . . I've talked to old-timers and listened to their reminiscences until I was bored out of my skull . . . I've gone through land title records and scoured the lists of cottagers' associations to try and locate people who were around at the time . . . I've driven all over the damn lake tracking them down . . . I've shown them pictures of my mother, my father, *your* father . . . I've gone through meteorological reports, lists of regatta winners, old registers at summer hotels and lodges, guest books at restaurants and in private homes . . . I've damn near combed the bottom of the lake, just in hopes of picking up some tiny, tiny scrap of useful information. And you don't want to listen!"

Lacey heard the intensity in his voice, saw the ferocity in his face, and at last his message reached her. For a few moments their eyes remained locked in recognition of why he had done all this. She knew, instinctively knew, that it was not for the sake of his mother.

"I'll listen," she whispered. "But I won't promise to believe."

And so he quickly told her all the other things he had learned—each minuscule detail, seemingly unimportant, with no detail enough in itself to disprove the story Aunt Edwina had told. For the most part, Gideon's research had been narrowed down to the year in question, the year of his conception. The name Jerrold—just Jerrold with no first name attached—had been found on a book of old receipts in a store. It wasn't a very common name, and the month was July. Hobie Hubbard's wife recalled Peggy Llewelyn when Gideon showed a photograph—"So pretty," she had said. She remembered seeing Peggy several times with a young man who was not Jacob Wynward. She couldn't remember the year or what the young man looked like, but she had the idea that they had been very much in love. She hadn't recognized the blurred snapshot, the only picture of his father that Gideon possessed, but she had conceded that it could be the same young man. "Though his hair wasn't near that dark," she had said.

"But it could have been streaked to a lighter color, like my own," Gideon pointed out to Lacey. She longed to believe him, but so far she had heard nothing that would even begin to convince her.

Someone else seemed to recall that Jacob Wynward had had a former college friend to visit at the Eyrie one time, someone by the name of Colin. That was the first name of Gideon's father, and combined with the evidence of the fuzzy photograph . . . "I think my father may have been visiting yours," Gideon guessed. "They *did* both go to Yale. In fact, it seems quite likely to me that your father introduced my parents."

There were a few other tiny details in support of

his theory. It was, he had often thought to himself over the course of the summer, like trying to reconstruct a picture of a prehistoric dinosaur from a fossilized footprint on rock, or a few shards of bone. Experts in the field did it all the time, and the absence of an entire skeleton didn't mean they were wrong. Often subsequent evidence proved the rightness of their guesses.

In the particular field of historical research, Gideon considered himself an expert, but this was the most tasking investigation he had ever undertaken. It had been an obsessive occupation, requiring fierce concentration and an ability to swallow disappointment. Frustration had often been the only reward for days of dogged work. Many times, when the research was particularly convoluted or obscure or unpleasant, only thoughts of the eventual prize had kept him going. He felt he deserved that prize now. With patience, perseverance, and the painstaking assembly of a score of tiny details, he'd worked up a convincing argument against Aunt Edwina's story.

"She told that lie," he finished forcefully, "simply to stop you from marrying me. I proposed in her hearing, if you remember. And she knew you were desperately in love. You *were* in love with me, Lacey. You *are* in love with me. Don't deny it, because I know that from a thousand small things. And I love you . . . oh, God, now can you see why I wanted this talk in a private place? Now that there's nothing to stop us—"

"There's everything to stop us, Gideon! Your wretched little clues aren't enough! Now please, please, *please* let me go."

At some point he had shifted his grip to her

shoulders, simply so she couldn't run away. She started to pull away now, and his hands tightened. "God, Lacey! Aren't you going to believe? The snapshot of my mother . . . that makes perfect sense now. And the note you told me about, that could too. Just put yourself in the picture—pretend you're my mother. She falls in love with a young man visiting Jacob Wynward, whom she's known for years. The young man leaves, perhaps for foreign parts—my father did do some traveling. She discovers she's pregnant. She doesn't know what to do. She thinks Jacob may be able to help . . . she hands him a hastily scribbled note, perhaps because there are other people around . . . your father saves it, and a few other things, because he once had romantic inclinations for my mother. Can't you see how it could have happened?"

"No!"

"Stop being so damn mule-headed! Just because you've believed something for eight years doesn't mean it's right."

"And just because you've believed something for one month—or one week—doesn't mean *that's* right!"

Gideon was breathing heavily. "In case you're in doubt about my intention in all this," he said heatedly, "I'm proposing again, right now. I intend to marry you, Lacey Wynward."

Lacey was in a storm of emotions, and the purposeful set of Gideon's mouth convinced her no more than his list of unimportant details had done. "I can't marry my own brother!" she cried.

Gideon's teeth gleamed in the dim light, but not in a smile. They were gritted and bared with animal ferocity. "Lacey! You are *not* my sister. I am *not* your brother. I refuse to believe it. There's nothing in heaven or on earth to prevent me from marrying you . . . loving you . . . having you. And by God, that's what I intend to do!"

"It's *sick* that you've been obsessed with this for a whole summer!" Her words were wild, perhaps dictated by the poison that had infected her own system for so long. "Go sleep with someone else, Gideon, and leave your sister alone!"

After his dogged, obsessive occupation of the summer, there was enough truth in those hurtful words to drive Gideon over a dangerous emotional brink. With swift and raging purpose, his mouth closed over Lacey's. She saw the dark message in his descending eyes, felt the anger and passion and frustration in his mouth as he tried to pry her lips apart. Her chest heaved and heat raced across the surface of her humid skin, but she had the strength of will to tear her face away, avoiding the intimacy.

And then, with frantic effort, she wrenched herself out of his hands altogether and ran. She wasn't sure of her direction—only that it took her away from Gideon. Flagstone paths crisscrossed the island, some lighted, some dark. She took the first of the lighted ones . . . and saw a small cabin ahead . . . and heard Gideon's ragged breathing closing in from behind. . . .

She entered the cabin and slammed the door. Fumbling in the dark, she could find no lock on it. She leaned against it when he pushed, but her strength was no match for his. In the next moment the door was flung wide and Gideon's tall frame filled the entrance, ominously silhouetted against the lights along the path.

"I'm not letting you get away so easily, Lacey. Not until we've had this out to the end!"

He reached for a switch, and a dim, dim light pervaded the interior of the cabin. Then, with a twist of a knob in the door handle itself, he located the lock that Lacey had not been able to find.

She looked around wildly. In the poorly illuminated interior, there were rows of wooden benches and very little else . . . no other exits, no other rooms. Why, in the name of all that was right, had she had to pick the sauna? There was no escape in here, only a greater danger. The sauna was not in operation, but the pre-storm humidity made her feel as if it were. The moisture of excessive heat and excessive effort and excessive emotion dampened her skin, and perhaps the steam of earlier saunas also lingered in the close, small space, adding to the effect.

Even though she had never been in a sauna before, in the murky workings of her mind the place had assumed erotic proportions beyond the telling. The determined desire that darkened Gideon's face promised no safety and no haven, as his arms had once done. And his state of near undress, the sheen of moisture over his tall, lithe, muscular frame, little concealed by the brief dark swimsuit, contributed to the volcanic sensations that assailed her. She backed away until her knees came in contact with a cedar bench, when she could retreat no farther.

The dark, dangerous passions in the humid atmosphere closed in like the lowering stormclouds outside. The forces of nature were mighty, inexorable, inescapable, and so was the force of Gideon's summer obsession, which had had one goal only—

to earn him the right to lay claim to Lacey Wynward. He felt he had done so. He knew she loved him. She couldn't deny him now!

He moved forward, his shadowed eyes fastened on Lacey. His obdurate mouth and his slow predatory advance caused shudders of expectation in her core.

He seized her, his hands shackling her slim shoulders, while he continued his protestations. His voice trembled and grew thick with emotion. "There's no wrong in the way I feel about you, Lacey. And no wrong in the way you feel about me . . . in the way you respond to me . . . in the way you love me."

"I don't," she protested, but the truth was otherwise and Gideon knew it with every fiber of his being.

"You do!" The assertion was ferocious, uttered through clenched teeth, as if the battering ram of raw elemental emotion could beat down her defenses where logic had failed. "You prove it every time you look at me, every time you touch me, every time you kiss me . . ."

The certainty that he was going to do so again caused a wild pounding of blood through her veins. Her palms were flattened against Gideon's bared, broad chest in an effort to prevent a greater closeness. She could feel the overwhelming power of him, the furnace heat of his flesh, and the insane tempo of her heart was echoed and answered by the thud of his. His heartbeat crashed against her fingers like stormwaves against a shore. Both were in the grip of strong primitive emotions, but Lacey was fighting for control of hers, and Gideon wasn't. His face was savage with the need to convince.

And so was Lacey's. "Don't touch me, Gideon! It's wrong!"

"Don't tell me there's wrong in this!"

Swiftly, his shadowy face descended. She arched her head away, hoping to evade his lips, only to feel them scorching across her throat. His hot mouth sought, claimed, demanded his right to possess. The explosiveness of his passion caused a wild, unwilling leaping of her flesh. Weakened and wanton in that moment, Lacey moaned to feel his sensuous savagery, and an irresistible lava flow of need poured through her lower limbs.

His mouth took her helplessly parted lips, and his tongue drove to dominate without request, recklessly demanding the reward she had sought to withhold. The sudden, surging depth of his commanding kiss took her by storm, suffocated her protests, obliterated thought.

His hands were all over her now, moving to discover the swell of her breasts, to mold her tender womanly flesh through the thin cotton. Finding too many obstacles to his sense of touch, he brushed his way downward to the edge of her loose blouse. His hand shook with impatience, for the unleashed need of many weeks consumed him. He insinuated his fingers at her waist, reaching up toward the fastening of her bra.

Lacey felt it being released, felt the swift seizure of a taut, trembling nipple. And then her blouse was pushed high to expose the thrust of her breasts, and Gideon's adamant lips were seeking possession of the tautened nipples. He felt her shuddering protest, but he also felt her passion, and so he used mouth, tongue, teeth—the weapons of arousal in a war against her reservations.

He clasped her close when she struggled, his warm chest clamped against breasts dampened by his lips. Lacey moaned while he muttered vehement love words against her mouth. "No power on earth can keep you from me . . . if you run from me I'll follow . . . if you refuse to listen to me I'll shout the story to the sky . . . if you refuse to touch me, I'll touch until you know it's right . . ." His hand delved beneath her loosened shorts, and his fingers tangled at her thighs. "Like this . . . and this . . . how can you tell me it's wrong?"

He was promising her heaven, and he was wooing her into hell. She twisted in an effort to free herself, but she was fighting the volcano of her own passion, too, and Gideon would not be deterred. His mouth offered torment and temptation . . . and then his fingers shifted urgently to her buttocks. A hand pressed her close against his thighs, so that she was unable to escape awareness of the great need that consumed him.

"And don't tell me there's wrong in this," he muttered in her ear, the vicious intensity of his voice venting some of his frustrated ardor. For Gideon, it was not enough to overpower her with the domination of his male sexuality. It was the surrender of her mouth and her mind and her heart that he wanted, the words of promise that would bind her to him for all time to come. He had felt Lacey's resistance and knew he had to stop, even though all nature and all the universe said it was right, right, right. . . .

The banging at the door of the sauna brought Gideon's impassioned embrace to a halt more quickly than he himself would have been able to do. Instantaneously he jerked away from Lacey.

And then came Debbie's bright voice: "Hey, you in there, whoever you are! Share the fun, huh? We all want in!"

Dashed back to realization, Lacey was already fighting with her bra straps, her fingers trembling because she had been far, far closer to capitulation than was good for her soul. Her few brief, fluttering struggles had been the last stand of desperation; she knew that given very little more in the way of encouragement, within moments she might have ceded to Gideon's tempestuous passion.

She was impressed that Gideon managed to remain calm under the circumstances. "Hold on, Deb," he called in an admirably casual voice. "We were just trying to figure out how the damn thing works."

Outside the door, Debbie giggled. "Knock it off, Gideon, you know exactly how to get the damn thing going. More likely you're trying to get the steam turned *off*. You and . . . is it Lacey Wynward in there? She wasn't on the boat ride."

With little choice in the matter, Gideon conceded that it was indeed Lacey. He switched on the steam, grabbed a towel from a shelf, and sat down on a bench near the door with the towel decently draped over the traitorous contours of his bathing suit. He watched intently while Lacey's fingers fumbled at her shorts. "We'll talk later," he muttered sotto voce.

"Hurry it up," Debbie urged. "It's starting to sprinkle out here. We want to steam up before the downpour starts, so we can run in the rain to cool off."

With those small delays, Lacey was perfectly decent when Gideon reached across to open the door. A half dozen towel-wrapped individuals spilled through the entrance. Lacey almost collided with someone in her haste to get out.

"What's the matter with her?" Debbie asked, staring at Lacey's fleeing figure.

"Modesty," Gideon said blandly. "I shouldn't have tried to talk her into it."

He would have followed Lacey at once, but he was still valiantly trying to fight the state of his arousal. Two minutes later, when he reached the place where her canoe had been pulled ashore, it was gone.

He dove into a channel now lashed with driving rain, cursing himself for not bringing his boat. Minutes later he was racing barefoot along the footpath to the Wynward cottage. Frenzy drove his feet over hard roots and small rocks he hardly felt, and occasional forks of jagged lightning lit his way.

But by the time he reached the Eyrie's boathouse, the Ditchburn was gone too.

Chapter Eleven

The thunderstorm had broken with a vengeance, but the dangers of the black night and the black water seemed no greater than the dangers Lacey had left behind. With visibility so badly restricted by the wall of driving rain, she could see little beyond the Ditchburn's running lights—white at the bow, red to port, green to starboard, all of them blurred by the downpour, pitching wildly up and down in the high waves.

Lacey's heart was in her mouth with every pitch and every yaw of the long, narrow vessel. But at least she had corrected the dangerous rolling of a few minutes before by turning the head directly into the wind, and her main fight now was to keep it aimed that way. Earlier, with the water driving hard at the broadside of the boat, each wave had seemed only a breathtaking moment away from swamping the hull altogether.

Lacey had risen to her feet to steer, and she had slowed the boat to a crawl to ride out the storm. At this point, able to see only a pitch-black hellhole ahead of her, she would not have dared to increase the speed. Nor would she have known which direction to take; she had no idea where she was. She had tried to aim for open lake, but somehow she had become lost in a maze of islands—which islands she wasn't sure. It wasn't the Wynward group; she had put that behind immediately after pulling away from shore.

The lightning had been frightening at first but now she welcomed it. Such few views as she had of the dark, close shorelines came only from the jagged, intermittent flashes that streaked down from the heavens, as if in righteous vengeance against the unnatural cravings she was attempting to flee. Several times the lightning had saved her from running aground.

At length the worst of the storm passed. The tempestuous wind began to fall, having brought a drop of many degrees in temperature. The thunder rolled into the horizon. The fury of the rain eased and settled into a straight, heavy downpour.

Lacey's tension began to ease a little as the pitch of the boat became less acute, but her nervousness grew again as the lightning flashes continued to fade with distance, no longer offering a beacon to her anxious eyes.

She had long since ceased to have any goal save that of keeping herself alive and the boat afloat, away from the hazards that loomed in those close black shores, where rocks often jutted up through the water. She knew the lake fairly well, but had never before tried to navigate at night, nor was the Ditchburn equipped for it. Traveling on island-strewn waters was risky, she knew, even on a clear night with a full moon. The shorelines, which were familiar and friendly by day, became treacherous traps by night, and the reflective navigation buoys could not be seen unless one shined a beacon directly at them. In her youth she had heard other people more skilled than she in navigation try to guess: was this a channel or an inlet? Was that an island or the mainland? Where was the buoy that marked shallow waters? Had they misinterpreted the chart they were trying to read by flashlight?

Tonight, with no chart, no moon, no stars, no strong searchlight beacon to probe the black secrets of the shores and the waters, navigation had become a matter of blind guessing. To come out on a night like this had been the action of a fool—a fool driven by a danger beyond reason. Lacey's fear of the night and the storm was no greater than her fear of the tempest of forbidden passion she had left behind.

She was thoroughly soaked, hair streaming, clothes sopping, rain blinding her eyes and running over her face. She hadn't taken time to raise the Ditchburn's torn canvas canopy in order to gain the little protection it would have offered. Nor had she taken time to retrieve any possessions from the cottage, except for a leather shoulderbag that contained car keys and other vital things. That sat on the seat beside her, also soaked. She had left a very great deal behind on the Eyrie—but not as much as she would have left behind if she'd stayed to listen to Gideon's persuasions. Had she done that, had she allowed herself to respond physically, she would have lost another part of a soul already deeply imperiled by her past.

The rain poured on, but the wind died more. Gradually the thunder rumbled into the very far distance. The slowly purring engine of the Ditchburn could once more be heard. By a last pale illumination of the lightning, she saw what might be a channel to open water and slowly headed toward it. But then the lightning ceased altogether, and Lacey didn't know which way to go. All around her was black, unending black. No cottage lights pricked the dark to warn of coming obstacles, leading her to believe she might indeed have reached open lake. But then she glanced around, squinting against the rain, and in all three hundred and sixty degrees of vision, there were no pinpricks of light at all. Possibly, no, probably, the storm had knocked out a main power line.

She tried to bring the motor down to a complete idle, and it stalled.

She pressed the starter without success. And again . . . and again.

Possibly some vital part was wet, possibly Lacey's distress had resulted in robbing her of such boating skills as she had, or possibly fate was simply taking more of its vengeance. At any rate, the engine didn't catch. She kept trying, but soon the battery grew weak. The running lights, operated by the boat's electrical system, began to fade. Lacey switched them off to wait for a few minutes, hoping the battery would recover a little of its juice. Then, with a silent prayer, she turned them on again and once more pressed the starter. The lights dimmed to nothing.

She tried to tell herself it was no less safe to drift in the dark than to drive, and perhaps that was true. But the total absence of illumination, the utter dominion of the wet darkness enveloping her, created a cold knot of terror in her stomach.

It was still raining, steadily and heavily, the sort of rain that might keep up for hours. She had no idea whether she had reached open lake or not. If she had, with no running lights, there was now a different danger, not only to herself but to others. Other boaters in the dark—if any were foolish enough to be out on a night like this—wouldn't be able to see her at all.

And then she thought of another concern. The bilge pump ran on the battery, too, and it had also stopped.

The battering of the waves had not helped the Ditchburn's ancient and rotting hull. The large leak might have grown larger. What with the steady continuing downpour and the spray that had poured over the gunwales a short time before, the boat must by now have shipped a fair amount of water. In the dark Lacey felt around until she found a lifebuoy, not the best and safest variety, but the seat-cushion kind. It was an old one, survivor of many years at the Eyrie. To her dismay, it already felt soggy and heavy with water. Groping, she could find no alternative that seemed to offer an improvement.

She strapped it to herself as best she could, then sat down on a sopping leather seat and huddled her arms together. Her dripping clothes clung to her like a second, soaked skin, offering no protection at all. She started to shiver, whether with nerves, with wet, or with chill she didn't know. She fought for calm, knowing that unless help happened upon her, there was nothing that could be done until dawn. She could only drift, and wait, and wait, and drift. . . .

Through the rain, Gideon had seen the tiny lights of the departing Ditchburn after his race to the main cottage. He had tried to shout at Lacey to come back, but his bellow had been lost in the howl of wind and the great voice of the thundering heavens. Again he had cursed himself for not coming by boat; but with the storm breaking, it hadn't occurred to him that she would actually be foolhardy enough to risk herself on the lake. Even the best of boatmen avoided nights like this.

The search since had been frantic, the first part of it through a dangerously wicked storm. But at least Gideon had a hand-held searchlight to help him, and a great deal of familiarity with night boating on this particular lake. He recognized the shorelines almost by osmosis, without even looking for landmarks.

He'd been searching for two hours. The rain was still steady, but slower. The night air was now cold. Gideon, although he still wore only his bathing suit, was spared the realization of exactly how cold it was. He was operating on adrenaline and inner heat generated by his fierce concern for Lacey. By now he knew she hadn't reached the public docks at Hubbard's Landing, which must have been her goal. Possibly, she'd found safe haven at some cottage, or possibly . . .

Gideon refused to let himself dwell too much on the possible. Lacey was, he told himself sternly, simply lost. At night it could happen even to a seasoned Muskoka-ite. And if she had foundered near an island, she would most surely have been able to reach shore.

With the same grim determination that had seen him through a summer of obsessive search, he simply kept looking. He shone his beam at docks where she might have taken shelter, he peered closely at rock projections that might rip through a boat's bottom, and always, at all times, he kept his eyes narrowed and eagle-sharp to watch for the telltale glimmer of a large boat's running lights.

He searched first through several groups of islands, knowing that the greatest dangers for a neophyte lay in the tangle of treacherous rocks and channels and hidden waterways. If she was out on the open lake, she would be far, far safer, although she might still be lost, drifting, waiting for morning. But he didn't think she was out there, or he would have spotted her lights.

Once or twice during his search he had raced to the public docks, simply to see if she'd arrived. Having searched another island group, he decided to do so again. This time he would call for others to join the search. Without hesitation, he veered toward the open lake. Once he was free of the perilous shores, he revved up to top speed.

The faint, faint sound that reached him through the roar of his engine might have been imagination, but something made Gideon's hand jam the shift and cut back to neutral. In an instant his searchlight was on. And then he heard the cry again, far louder now—in fact, very, very close. The searchlight moved over the near waters and there it was, the Ditchburn, that grand old dame of the lakes, sitting a little low in the water, but with its mahogany hull still looming higher than his.

He circled slowly, coming back alongside the larger, longer boat. His light picked out Lacey's pale face, her soaked slicked hair, her huddled arms. A lumpy old lifebuoy cushion, faded with age, was tied across her chest. She had risen to her feet to greet him, and she was shivering uncontrollably. She looked as though she was on her last legs.

Gideon thought he had never seen anything more unspeakably beautiful in his life. "Lacey, thank God—" The sudden obstruction in his throat prevented him from saying more.

Lacey gave him a wan, wet smile. She thought she'd never seen anything more beautiful, either, than the gleam of pale light catching the hills and hollows of that lean, familiar face. For once there were no uncomfortable undercurrents in her reaction. She was simply, purely, and unimaginably relieved. Twice before Gideon had roared past in his boat, in ignorance of her desperate attempts to hail him. She had begun to think there would be no rescue before morning. And each time, her heart had been in her throat with the fear that Gideon might run her down at full speed in the dark and put his own life in jeopardy.

Her lips were stiff with cold, her facial muscles numb with exhaustion. It was a moment before she managed to form a greeting. She lifted a thumb.

"Hi," she said. "Going my way?" They were the same words she had used eight years before.

"If you're going mine," Gideon answered, his voice choked with deep, heartfelt emotion.

It took time to reach the Eyrie, for a large boat could not simply be left drifting in the lake. It offered too many hazards for other boaters. Arranging the mechanics of the tow was slow, and half an hour passed before Lacey and Gideon reached the warmth and haven of the cottage. By then coldness had reached down into the very marrow of their bones.

Lacey was in a state of immense weariness by the time they reached the island. She was tired, tired, tired beyond the point of caring about anything. Still wrapped in a canvas dropsheet that had been found in Gideon's boat, she sank down onto the floor of the boathouse and watched with dull, dazed eyes while he secured the two boats. The sullen heat, the wild storm, the scare of the long wait in the dark, and then the wetness that had turned to numbing cold—each of these things had taken its toll, along with all the emotions she had suffered through in recent hours. The stuffing was simply knocked out of her. If Gideon wanted to take masterful charge, she was quite prepared to let him do it. She didn't even object when he swept her into his arms and carried her up the creaky old stairs.

Nor did she object when he strode into the bathroom, ran a hot bath, and helped her into it. Her one feeble objection subsided when Gideon simply started stripping her without ado, his hands as impersonal as a doctor's. The bath was a balm. She felt as if she didn't have an erotic bone in her body, or indeed any bone at all. She was limp in every limb, hardly able to remain upright while he toweled her. Her hair was still wet, but there was no help for that; it would have taken too long to dry. She was so, so tired.

And when he lifted her to carry her to bed, she simply collapsed into his arms and allowed it. As her head struck a towel-covered pillow, she remembered thinking, *It's a good thing I trust him. Dear, dear, Gideon.*

Trust was a very subjective thing. It was remarkable how little she felt when she woke the following morning to find that she had slept beside him, naked but for the bed coverings draped over her, half enclosed by his arm. She could feel the weight of it across the blanket over her breast.

She turned rigid, her immediate thought the very worst. And then, in the instant before she would have leaped from the bed, she felt the blankets that separated the length of their bodies and saw that he was clothed, and gradually the fear subsided.

He was still asleep. He must have returned to the bunkhouse at some point during the night, for he was fully dressed in a loose brown sweater and old cords. He had slept on top of the covers, one arm flung over Lacey and the blankets that kept her warm. No longer assailed by the emotional trauma of the previous evening, she could think more rationally now. With a small sense of surprise, considering the events at the Hallorans' party, she found that she really did trust him. And the bed coverings, lying like a sword of honor between them, proved that her trust was not misplaced.

With a restlessness that suggested his dreams were not easy ones, Gideon groaned in his sleep and shifted, moving the arm that pinioned her in place. Lacey was free to slide out of bed without disturbing him, and yet she stayed.

Scarcely daring to breathe, she turned her head and allowed her yearning eyes to search his face. Had she been able to do so with impunity, she would have reached up to touch the hollows where his lashes fell . . . the lick of hair that fell across his forehead . . . the tiny, slow pulse at his temple . . . the faint, unrazored stubble of the morning . . . the shadowed hollow at the base of his throat.

She permitted her eyes these liberties because she knew it might be for the very last time. It was a weakness; but it was a weakness that would have to last a lifetime. And the expression in her eyes was not that of desire, but the great darkness of a deep, quiet sorrowing. After today she would not see Gideon again.

His anguished words about following her had been rashly spoken and soon repented. Looking at him with love aching like an open wound in her heart, she now remembered that he'd told her so, during the long trip back to the Eyrie. She had been benumbed at the time and his chastened apology had hardly reached her, but she could hear him now in the caverns of her memory: "I'd do nothing—nothing!—to harm you, darling. I love you, Lacey. I'm not your brother; I'm as sure of that as if my mother herself had told me. But if you refuse to believe . . . if you refuse to accept . . . how could I force myself upon you in any way? I spoke wildly, I acted wildly tonight, but I won't act wildly again. I swear it! I'll never, never again give you cause to run away from me."

Remembering it now, she felt that his apology

was sincere. He had been in a highly emotional state during the encounter at the Hallorans'—not really himself. And perhaps it was little wonder. With a whole summer of intensive research behind him, he must have found it very frustrating when his theories failed to convince her. He truly believed they weren't brother and sister; she knew that. She ached to believe it too. In her mind, hoping against hope that she would find some reason to change her stand, she went over each of the details he had presented to her. They weren't enough to counteract the desperate little message in the note Peggy Llewelyn had written so long ago. Gideon might have convinced himself, but he hadn't convinced Lacey.

And that started another train of speculation, one as difficult to resist as the temptation to memorize his face. It was a line of thought wonderful yet terrible, awful yet awe-inspiring.

Gideon loved her. He loved her. *He loved her.* Not as he ought to, not as a brother should, but as she loved him. He wanted to marry her—marry her! And that in itself was a source of wonder. Of wonder, and of fear, and of bittersweet longing for a destiny denied to them by the cruel hand of fate.

And when her heart grew too large with the pain and the futility and the beauty of being loved, she slipped quietly from the bed, silently gathered some clothes from a drawer, and left the room.

Chapter Twelve

_L_ acey now felt less urgency to leave, although her decision to put the Eyrie and Gideon behind her had not been in any way changed. But at least she could leave, she thought, in more orderly fashion. In the desperate night flight she had felt impelled to make, she had done none of the usual cottage close-up things—the packing of clothes, the stripping of beds, the final fastening of windows and shutters, the laying out of mousetraps, and last but not least the emptying of the refrigerator.

Not wanting to disturb Gideon, she quietly set about doing some of these tasks. She wanted to be off in good time in order to see the real estate agent and pay a parting visit to her aunt, but she had awakened early and would be able to accomplish all that was necessary around the cottage within two or three hours. After a summer of loving care and only one occupant, the cottage was neither messy nor unclean.

Soon the kitchen, the biggest job, was done. Supplies that would not winter well were packed into cardboard boxes, and she had put aside some of the perishables for Gideon's use, as he would undoubtedly be staying on at the bunkhouse until a little later in the season. She'd eaten a small breakfast, emptied the cupboards, cleaned out the fridge, and placed charcoal inside to absorb unpleasant odors—a trick she remembered from many summers ago. A large pot of coffee remained on the hob, along with fruit and cereal for Gideon's breakfast, something she felt she couldn't fail to offer.

All the small rituals of sorting and discarding, mundane though they were, helped Lacey to do some sorting in her mind, and the mental sorting led to a gradual return of inner peace. Had she given in to the temptation of yielding to Gideon's convictions, who else but herself would have known? To the rest of the world, they were not brother and sister, and never would be. Those who might have known the truth—Gideon's parents, her own father, Aunt Edwina—were either dead or incapable of understanding. The only remaining barriers to full, free love were all in Lacey's conscience, for certainly there were no impediments in Gideon's mind. Yet, despite all the weakness she felt for him, she hadn't been weak. She hadn't agreed to enter into a relationship that beckoned, lured, wooed her with its fatal, forbidden sweetness. She had said no to a temptation so great that it dwarfed anything else in her imagination.

And so it was during the hours of cottage closing,

at the end of the long, slow, seductive summer, that Lacey's understanding of herself came full circle. The sins were still in her mind, and perhaps her flesh was weak—but at least her spirit was willing to submit to the stern, unpalatable taboos of her conscience.

After this day, she felt, her deep, deep guilt and shame and self-doubt could at least be tempered with some self-respect.

She left her own room to the last, because she thought Gideon needed his sleep. During the minutes when she had lain beside him, she had felt he looked exhausted. His restless slumber had been disturbed by frowns and twitches and involuntary groans, all of which suggested that he wasn't sleeping well.

When there were no tasks left except her personal packing, she finally returned to her own room. But Gideon wasn't there, only a note pinned to the pillow. "The cottage offer still stands," it said. "If you see my agent, you can settle the whole thing any time it suits you. The price is the same. When I mentioned a different offer, I was speaking of another one altogether—and that offer still stands too. You know what I mean. Yours, G."

He didn't seem to be anywhere else in the cottage. Lacey was still occupied in a room-to-room search when she heard the rumble of a boat starting up—Gideon's. The previous evening he had left it in the boathouse, and she recognized its particular smooth sound. It certainly wasn't the inoperable Ditchburn.

She ran to a window in time to see the orange boat backing out of its slip. And Gideon, standing like a stern figurehead at the wheel . . . even from this distance, she could see that his eyes were deeply etched with dark circles and that his jaw was set into a hard, determined line.

She tried to swallow the hurt occasioned by his wordless departure. It troubled her that he would simply awaken and leave without saying good-bye. She decided that he must have felt incapable of confronting her after the happenings of the previous evening. And perhaps, after all, that was best.

But it meant calling the marina for a ride to the mainland, for without Gideon to transport her, she would need Hobie Hubbard's help. She placed the call from the phone that had been installed earlier in the summer, not in Aunt Edwina's room, but in the living room, with an extension at her own bedside.

Hobie agreed to arrive within the hour. "Figgered to be there anyways," he said, somewhat to Lacey's surprise. "Mr. Jerrold called jest a little while ago an' tole me to come an' fetch the big boat."

"Oh?" Lacey realized that Gideon must have placed the call while she had been working in the kitchen, where she wouldn't have been able to hear him.

"Yup. Said she was sinking in the slip, an' the bilge pump knocked out. She was out in the storm, he said, an' the bottom musta been banged about some, mebbe 'cause of the waves, mebbe on a rock. Said he spent most o' the night with a hand pump, emptying the water she'd shipped. Safe now, he reckoned—fer a time. But he tole me I'd best git there soon, afore she goes down."

No wonder Gideon had looked exhausted! Lacey

was touched that he had taken such trouble for the old boat. Also, having heard of the seriousness of the Ditchburn's condition, she shuddered slightly to think of the possible outcome, had Gideon not found her drifting in the dark. The life jacket had not seemed very trustworthy, and she wasn't a wonderful swimmer. Nor would she have known which direction to swim.

Hobie rambled on, supplying more information. "Tole me to give that Ditchburn the works, Mr. Jerrold did. New bottom, new engine mebbe, new canopy, refinish the top. Sure be good to see that ole boat saved. Used to be the finest on the lake back in its day—an' I reckon it will be again, after a winter's work."

So the magnificent old boat was going to see better days again. The knowledge filled Lacey with a warm gratitude that the Ditchburn would now have an owner who cared, an owner like Gideon. The stately antique, even with all its old-age troubles, had wormed its way into her heart, just as the cottage itself had done. Gideon, she felt, would rescue them both. Passingly, she regretted that he hadn't bought the property with all its various belongings in time to save the treasured old Dippy, along with everything else.

After Lacey hung up, she spent some time transporting boxes and suitcases down to the boathouse, ready for the trip to shore. And then, with everything done, there were some minutes of nostalgia as she walked around and said her last farewells to each of the things she loved.

"Someone else will have to love you from now on," she said wistfully to the moosehead. And each small thing received its own silent good-bye, but when she came to the casement window, she turned her eyes away. All that was in the past.

After a moment of indecision she lifted the picture of all the Wynwards from over the mantel, deciding to take it with her. Her father's photograph would only serve to remind Gideon of unhappy things, and the other portraits would be of no interest to him whatsoever. Perhaps there were other family photographs she should take? Aunt Edwina had a vast collection of snapshots around somewhere . . . now, where had she kept it?

After a moment of thinking, Lacey remembered. In one of Aunt Edwina's drawers, which had been subjected to a clean-out along with everything else back at the beginning of the summer, there had been a large old dress box that bore the mark of a Paris couturier long since forgotten. The box had been chock-full of assorted summer snapshots and other yellowed mementos. Lacey had opened it long enough to see a few of the things. A photograph of Aunt Edwina, posed on the dock beside the Ditchburn, with Lacey's parents and Lacey herself as a child . . . a few waxed autumn leaves . . . a picture of Lacey in her seventeenth summer, sitting in the old Dippy, squinting in the sun, with Gideon standing on the dock holding the painter line. Those had been some of the memories in view on the topmost layer.

At the time of finding the large box, because Lacey had not yet come to terms with the past, it had been very disconcerting for her to see that picture of Gideon and herself, taken at a time when she had still been in the bloom of innocence and young love, ignorant of their close kinship. And so she had closed the lid and returned the box to its niche. But with some of the terrible pain of that year now accepted, she felt she could bear to go through the contents. And certainly, Aunt Edwina's faded mementos would not be of much interest to anyone outside of the family.

Lacey went and retrieved the dress box, planning to take it back to Pittsburgh for future sorting. However, as she was still waiting for Hobie Hubbard to put in an appearance, and because there was no point in collecting useless clutter, she started to leaf through the old snapshots, thinking that some of them might go directly into the garbage. Most of them did. Lacey sat in one of the big armchairs she'd slipcovered herself, with the box on her lap and a wastepaper basket at her feet, disposing of many Muskoka memories she didn't care to keep.

She saved the snapshots of her parents; a few of Aunt Edwina at various stages in her life; a few of herself as a child. The autumn leaves went into the trash, along with herself in the Dippy, and snapshots of many people she didn't recognize. For some of those shots, the only guide was the brief little notation of the year and at times the person's identity, written on the photograph's back in Aunt Edwina's spidery hand. As Lacey worked her way down through the box, the photographs grew older. During years farther in the past, when Aunt Edwina had not been so pitifully short of money, she had been much more active with a camera. The snapshots for those years were far more plentiful, but the memories were also more obscure.

Most of them went with the discards. And then . . .

Suddenly the memories were not obscure at all. Lacey's heart seemed to freeze as she stared at the snapshot in her hands. Peggy Llewelyn's dimpled face smiled back at her. The year noted on the back was . . .

"The right year," Lacey whispered to herself, with a stunned realization of the great treasure she might hold in her lap.

Her heart started to beat in jackhammer rhythm as she leafed past the next photograph, and the next, and the next, in a search for something she hardly even dared to name to herself. And then again, another photograph stopped her, and this time it was of pretty Peggy Llewelyn with a young brown-haired man. They were sitting in the Ditchburn, then in the prime of condition and gleaming with the fine mahogany patina of loving care. Lacey's father was in the picture too—at the wheel. It was a clear, finely detailed photograph, taken with a good camera.

With trembling fingers, Lacey turned the photograph over. The date was right, but there was no notation of the young man's name. And Lacey had no idea of what Gideon's father looked like. *He* would know of course, but Lacey was filled with the urgent need to know herself—instantly, at once, without waiting for anyone else's verdict.

Now frantic with urgency, she pawed through the photographs still in the box, scattering the discards on the floor with no thought for tidiness.

And then again she stopped. Peggy Llewelyn wasn't in this latest photograph, but the young man was . . . at least, Lacey thought it was the same young man . . . maybe, maybe, maybe . . .

Actually the snapshot was of two young men, on a sailboat in the water. It had been taken from some distance, so the features were not very clear. Lacey thought she recognized one of the men as her father. She turned and read the caption on the back, and knew her search was over. Gideon's guesses had been right.

The orange boat swerved into the dock an hour later, and within moments Gideon came crashing up the stairs.

He burst into the living room, where she was still sitting in a daze of wonderment, in too much of a tremble to clean up the clutter that surrounded her. At Gideon's advent, she rose to her feet, love and acceptance of love glowing luminously in her eyes.

"Lacey, thank God you haven't gone! Hobie told me you were still here. Lacey, I've got to talk to you, at once. I have a new clue. I swear I'm not your brother. I swear it! And if this doesn't prove it to you—"

"I believe you," she said simply, before he even had a chance to explain.

That threw Gideon off stride. He came to a halt halfway across the room, and for a moment he stared at her as if it were he who had turned incredulous. "How did you know?" he asked in a cracked, curious voice. "Did Gladdie Brenner phone you?"

She would have moved toward him but suddenly she felt tongue-tied, awkward about telling him that it was her own last-minute search that had convinced her, not his dogged summer-long persistence.

"No, she didn't phone," Lacey said, remaining where she was. Her face was warm with all the feelings she had so long tried to conceal. Now it didn't matter if Gideon knew she loved him. "Should she have?"

"No . . . she wouldn't have known she had anything important to say. God! She's been sitting on a gold mine of information all summer long, and if I'd only thought to question her I could have saved myself a helluva lot of legwork. You'd better take this sitting down, Lacey. It's proof positive as far as I'm concerned." He uttered a roar of a laugh, the triumphant sound of a man in a delirium of happiness, and said something that Lacey didn't understand at all. "My God, I've been looking at the shadows of fossilized footprints all this time, with the whole damn dinosaur sitting practically under my eyes!"

Lacey sat down. There was no mistaking the gleam of victory in Gideon's eye, and she didn't wish to deny him the pleasure of making his triumphant revelation, whatever it might be. "What did Gladdie Brenner say?"

Gideon drew in a deep breath. "First I'll tell you that I went to the hospital today, right after I left here. When you wouldn't listen to my theories, I swore to myself I'd sit by your aunt's bedside till the moment she expired—well, barring the times when the hospital wouldn't have me there at all. It seemed like a desperate hope, but it was the last hope I could think of. It's days since she's recognized me. But I kept thinking she might say something, drop some small clue in her ramblings. Part of me, to be honest, has been wanting to physically shake the truth out of her all summer long. And I think I almost would have several times, if I hadn't been so sure the shaking would also do her in completely, and with it maybe my hopes. I'm angry with her, Lacey—angry because she told that lie with full knowledge of what she was doing."

Since finding the photograph of Gideon's father —and a few others also in the box—Lacey had come to the same conclusion. Aunt Edwina had claimed that Colin Jerrold had not been in Muskoka during the summer of Gideon's conception, and yet he very patently had been, and in the month of July too. The dates on the backs of the photographs proved it. In fact, by now Lacey was sure that Gideon's father must have been staying as a guest at the Eyrie, and Aunt Edwina had most certainly known of his presence. All those notations had been in her own handwriting, and there had been one snapshot of the two of them together. Colin Jerrold's name had been written in full on the back of that one, along with a brief notation: Jacob's friend. There had also been a shot of Colin and Peggy arm-in-arm, with a gazebo in the background and Jacob Wynward sitting cross-legged at their feet, his arm around Lacey's mother. So she had been visiting too! And all of those snapshots had been taken in the one summer, the right summer, even the right month.

But for the time being, Lacey kept those glorious secrets to herself. "What did Gladdie Brenner say to you?"

"First I'll tell you how it came about. She asked if you were going to be in to see your aunt today, and I said I wasn't sure, although you probably would be. I told her you were leaving at once for Pittsburgh."

Gideon had walked over to the mantel and was leaning against it, his posture indolent, his arms folded. But there was no denying that the expression on his face was decidedly smug, as if he was about to make an important pronouncement. "And then?" Lacey prompted.

"And then," Gideon said in a slow, carefully articulated voice, "then she asked me, rather hesitantly, if you and I were going to get married."

"Married?" whispered Lacey, stunned although she hadn't thought Gideon could possibly say anything that would surprise her.

"Yes, married." Gideon laughed again, joyously, tilting his head back a little, looking heavenward as if in great thanks to the powers that be. Then, sobering, he returned to his explanations. "It goes right back to something Gladdie remembers from the beginning of the summer, Lacey, when your aunt was still having the occasional reasonably lucid spell. She told Gladdie you'd been waiting all these years for me to make my fortune. And now that I *had*, your aunt Edwina said . . . well . . ." He paused to give conscious drama to his words. "Now that I had, she told Gladdie, there was nothing to stop you from making a suitable match."

It took a few moments for Lacey to assimilate that. If Aunt Edwina had made a statement like that, she most certainly must have known there were no blood ties that would serve as an impediment to marriage.

"Gladdie hadn't repeated it earlier," Gideon went on, "because she thought the two of us didn't look as though there was a damn thing going on between us. She believed it was just another of your aunt's wilder imaginings."

"I wonder if that's why Aunt Edwina kept rambling on about weddings," Lacey mused with a certain amount of awe.

Gideon nodded. "I imagine so. And you know— the odd thing is, I was afraid of that at the time. I had the notion she'd decided I was a good match after learning my pseudonym. I believe that may have been why she was so anxious to speak to you when you first arrived in Muskoka. She wanted to tell you the truth."

"I wonder," Lacey said slowly, but the real wonderment was in her heart.

"I imagine that could also have something to do with her going on about fixing up the cottage and the boats, and a few of her other dreams of glory. In her head, I think she believed that my money— such as it is—was about to restore the Wynward family fortunes, her own included. Of course, you have to realize, it couldn't possibly do that. Nobody's *that* rich these days, and certainly not me."

Lacey smiled. "It was a bit of a pipe dream for her to tell someone we were getting married, when we hadn't seen each other for eight years."

"Half your aunt's life has been pipe dreams," Gideon said softly. "But this one . . . this one time, her pipe dream was real." He moved a little closer to Lacey and then halted, his eyes warm as they searched her shining face. "Do you think you can manage to get married without five hundred guests, two boxcars of rose petals, and thirty cases of vintage champagne?"

Lacey laughed, feeling gloriously giddy. Aunt

Edwina with her sad faults and old-fashioned values, living in a dream world that no longer existed, hoping for a restoration of a past that couldn't ever come again . . . it was Aunt Edwina who had committed the great original sin. But today Lacey was prepared to forgive anyone.

The moment of laughter brought a quick reaction as tears of pure happiness welled and trembled in her luminous eyes. "I think I could manage to get married wrapped in a canvas dropsheet with a case of chicken pox," she said as she rose and walked into Gideon's waiting arms.

They stayed on in Muskoka through an autumn that turned to flame and orange and gold, when nature's glories seemed but the mirror of a happiness that grew more vivid with each passing day.

Lacey's Aunt Edwina passed away peacefully shortly after her ninetieth birthday. She was not to witness or know about the marriage she had first conspired to stop, and at the very end had dreamed of helping to accomplish. By then, Lacey had accorded her some true forgiveness—not total forgiveness, because it was hard to fully forget those years of undeserved guilt and shame she had suffered through. And yet, perhaps Aunt Edwina had truly believed it was her duty to prevent the marriage of a seventeen-year-old niece who had been entrusted to her care.

But real forgiveness, full forgiveness, followed some other discoveries.

Another clue turned up unsought, at the bottom of Aunt Edwina's box of mementos—a clue that might or might not account for her tragically misguided lie. It was a very, very old love letter, written before the turn of the century. Its author had been Jack Llewelyn, first of the Llewelyns to come to the Muskoka lakes; its recipient had been Lacey's great-great-grandmother, Abigail Lacey, wife of the first Wynward and Aunt Edwina's mother. The letter was as brittle as old parchment, its edges crumbled with age and much handling. It was musty with faint perfume, as if it had been saved and treasured, hidden in a drawer amidst lavender-scented sachets. Aunt Edwina, Lacey thought, must have found it years ago, after Abigail Lacey Wynward's death.

"What do you think, Gideon?" Lacey asked after reading him the old, poignant letter that spoke of a hopeless, tragic love.

"That we're—what would it be, second cousins, as the result of some illicit passion years ago? What does it matter? That's a very permissible relationship. Come here and I'll show you how permissible it is."

"No, wait, Gideon. I didn't mean I thought we were related." True, the crumbling letter might have explained a vague similarity in eye color several generations later, but Lacey didn't think so. Her small venture into historical guesswork had suggested a different rationale. "I was talking about something else. You see, there's another thing I found . . ."

"I won't listen to another word. You've become too damn obsessed with this hunt into the past. And believe me, I had more than enough of it this summer. Mmm. You know something? You smell of lavender, just from touching that letter

. . . and pine needles, and spruce trees, and crunchy autumn leaves . . . and all those wonderful things . . ."

They were lying on a soft bed of fallen needles, decayed and grown spongy with the passage of the years. Much had changed, but this place hadn't. It was a small clearing halfway between the cottage and the bunkhouse, a place where they had lain years before, looking up through the dark silhouettes of the tall trees.

"Gideon! Wait . . ." He was nibbling at her throat, delving into all its soft hollows en route to the mouth he now knew so well. "You see, I think there's a reason that the brother and sister story occurred to Aunt Edwina . . ."

"Do you know, you have the most erotic little pulse down here," he murmured against the little space between her collarbones. "When you talk, it moves. It's a very, very sexy little part of you I've never fully appreciated before. Keep talking, Lacey. I want to appreciate some more."

Lacey disobeyed, stopping her chatter because he wasn't really listening. And she didn't want to talk, when there were better things to do with her mouth. She wound her arms around his neck and pulled his face toward hers. "Oh, Gideon," she marveled, "I love you more than I can tell."

"And I love you," he murmured. He looked down at her luminous face, his eyes deep and warm with a love that went far beyond passion. "In fact, you're an obsession with me, Lacey Wynward Jerrold, and it's going to take me a lifetime of research to prove the way I feel. At the moment I'm researching lips . . . very, very thoroughly . . ."

And after he had spent a little time making good his words, he muttered against her mouth, "I adore you to distraction, Lacey. Did I ever tell you that?"

"Only about a thousand times today." And after that, there was a long sweet lull filled only with the soft moans and whispers of lovers, and the sound of crunching pine needles.

And so it was some time before Lacey finished the tale of her own small foray into research. Later, when the time was right and they sat musing and dreaming in front of a leaping log fire, she told Gideon of the other mementos she had found, not in the large box, but in a small velvet-lined pouch among her aunt's most personal things. In the ribbon-tied pouch had been Aunt Edwina's old dance cards, with one particular name most often written in the blanks. There was a pressed rose that crumbled to the touch. There were also a few cherished photographs of Gideon's great-grandfather and namesake, Gideon Llewelyn, son of Jack. And there was a small bundle of chaste, respectful letters written seventy years before, when the century was young. In them, that Gideon of long ago had touchingly declared his love for young Edwina Wynward.

In the very last of his letters, Gideon Llewelyn had told of his intention to ask for Edwina's hand in marriage. And after that, there had been no more.

And Aunt Edwina had saved those love notes and mementos all these long years . . . she must have loved him too. Yet nothing had come of that old romance. Why not? Was it because she was her mother's daughter, and he was his father's son?

If so, it was a dark secret—a tragic secret out of a

tragic past. The real truth might never be known. All the same, tears were standing in Lacey's eyes when she finished telling Gideon her tentative conclusions. Because the story was so like her own, but without the final happiness, it had touched very close to her heart. "It's so sad," she said. "That old, doomed love . . . I think Aunt Edwina must have been very unhappy then. I wonder if that's why other things, trivial things, became so important to her as the years passed by."

"That's an old love story, Lacey," Gideon said quietly when he had listened through to the end. "It might explain why that particular invention occurred to your aunt, but it doesn't forgive what she did to you—and to me."

And then, because he felt the soft sorrowing in her, he pulled her head against his chest and smoothed the long black hair that, to his prejudiced eyes, gleamed like no other hair in the world. It was a black lake lapped by moonlight . . . but then, to him, it was not only her hair that made Lacey a woman beyond compare.

"I suppose you're right," Lacey agreed with a sigh. And yet, with a heart full to overflowing with happiness and love, she could no longer find it in herself to hold too much against Aunt Edwina, who had had so little of both.

The last small epilogue to the summer took place on the day they left Muskoka. Lacey had been doing a cottage close-up for the second time. On this occasion it was considerably more complex than the first, because for several weeks the cottage had had two very lazy occupants, both with a good deal of loving to catch up on. The bunkhouse had had to be cleaned out, too, so there was a considerable amount to be transported to the mainland. Gideon had taken the bulk of the load in the orange boat while Lacey stayed behind to do a few final things—for the most part, the rituals of farewell.

"Next summer you'll get looked after," she fervently promised the moosehead. So would the casement window, the roof, and about a hundred other things. Even with all the loving and lazing, Lacey and Gideon had found time to talk about a few other things. A good part of it had concerned generations of the future, not of the past. They had both agreed that two, three—or possibly four—small occupants would be needed to help fill some of the Eyrie's bedrooms in future years.

In October the lake was virtually empty of cottagers, so when Lacey heard boat sounds in the distance, she guessed it had to be Gideon. And yet, as the sounds neared there was a difference to them . . . a difference she recognized very well.

She was down on the dock when he arrived, the last few possessions piled beside her, ready to go. Her face was glowing. Why hadn't Gideon told her it was he who'd bought the Dippy?

The little disappearing propeller boat looked wonderful, spanking new with varnish and tender loving care. The distinctive putt-putt-putt of its motor was music to the ears. But to Lacey the most wonderful part about it was that Gideon had bought it for her, had it rebuilt for her, saved it as a surprise for her. He had done it to help her pay her marina bill; he had done it because he had instinctively known she would be sad to part with the old boat; but most of all, he had done it because he loved her, he loved her, he loved her. . . .

She knew these things with every gloriously happy bone in her body.

To her it was such a big, important gesture that she simply couldn't find immediate words to express how she felt. Gideon pulled in beside the dock and left the motor chugging. There was no reason she had to speak, because from the warm look in his eyes, it was clear that he knew exactly how she felt.

These happy tears, she felt, were becoming too much of a habit. And so her lips curved into a tentative smile as she raised her thumb in a hitchhiker's gesture. "Going my way?" she asked softly.

"If you're going mine," he said.

"I always will," Lacey promised softly.

Coming Next Month

Something Lost, Something Gained
by Carole Halston

Megan had been nervous about her big fashion writing assignment in the Caribbean, but when she found out her photographer partner was Case Ballantine, her ex-husband, she knew her toughest challenge would be to win him back to her side.

Firebird by Margaret Ripy

Three years before, Lindsey had refused to give up her career as a prima ballerina to follow Brazilian tycoon Jared St. Martin to the Amazon. Now Jared was back—and this time Lindsey knew she'd find it impossible to resist his fire.

End of Illusion by Amanda Lee

Kate had a ten-year-old son who needed a man's influence. Morgan Chandler had a teen-aged daughter in need of a woman's hand. Morgan's proposal that they become a family was tempting, but did he long for her as a woman as well as a wife?

Coming Next Month

Dream Of Yesterday by Nancy John

Kirstie had been too young when she first loved Adam Prescott. When they finally met again, another woman came to claim him. But Adam still wanted Kirstie more than any woman—and he was determined to have her.

Hearts In Exile by Ann Hurley

Cally and Jesse had shared many a madcap adventure while growing up on the Texas coast. Years later, they met again on a faraway shore. But how could their love last when one heart was in exile, too proud to look homeward?

Male Order Bride by Carolyn Thornton

Rafe Chancellor had besieged Lacey Adams with a barrage of whimsical messages and gifts just to convince her to date him. He soon won Lacey's heart, but was this charming man also game for an old-fashioned commitment?

£1.10 each

139 ☐ A HARD BARGAIN
Carole Halston

140 ☐ WINTER OF LOVE
Tracy Sinclair

141 ☐ ABOVE THE MOON
Antonia Saxon

142 ☐ DREAM FEAST
Fran Bergen

143 ☐ WHEN MORNING COMES
Laurey Bright

144 ☐ THE COURTING GAME
Kate Meriwether

145 ☐ SHINING HOUR
Pat Wallace

146 ☐ BY THE BOOK
Carolyn Thornton

147 ☐ APRIL ENCOUNTER
Gena Dalton

148 ☐ LEGACY OF FIRE
Lucy Gordon

149 ☐ APPALACHIAN SUMMER
Eva Claire

150 ☐ LEFTOVER LOVE
Janet Dailey

151 ☐ A LOVE SONG AND YOU
Linda Shaw

152 ☐ GENTLE POSSESSION
Melodie Adams

153 ☐ THE TANGLED WEB
Tracy Sinclair

154 ☐ A RULING PASSION
Doreen Owens Malek

155 ☐ SOFTLY AT SUNSET
Anne Lacey

156 ☐ TELL ME NO LIES
Brooke Hastings

157 ☐ FORBIDDEN SUMMER
Abra Taylor

158 ☐ THE MIRROR IMAGE
Maggi Charles

159 ☐ IN A PIRATE'S ARMS
Elaine Camp

160 ☐ ISLAND ROGUE
Linda Wisdom

161 ☐ THE HEART KNOWS BEST
Sodra Stanford

162 ☐ FIRST IMPRESSIONS
Nora Roberts

All these books are available at your local bookshop or newsagent, or can be ordered direct from the publisher. Just tick the titles you want and fill in the form below.

Prices and availability subject to change without notice.

SILHOUETTE BOOKS, P.O. Box 11, Falmouth, Cornwall.

Please send cheque or postal order, and allow the following for postage and packing:

U.K. – 50p for one book, plus 20p for the second book, and 14p for each additional book ordered up to a £1.63 maximum.

B.F.P.O. and EIRE – 50p for the first book, plus 20p for the second book, and 14p per copy for the next 7 books, 8p per book thereafter.

OTHER OVERSEAS CUSTOMERS – 75p for the first book, plus 21p per copy for each additional book.

Name ....

Address ....

....